The Friends I've Never Met

A Screenplay
by Heather Grace Stewart

Book 3 - Love Again Series

The Friends I've Never Met
by Heather Grace Stewart

Book 3 - Love Again Series

Published by Graceful Publications, 2017
Second edition December 2020

NOTE: This screenplay is 120 pages (approx. 2 hours screen time) as a Final Draft file, however, to accommodate the spine of this book and to ease your reading, the book has a wider left margin and at times I've left some spaces between scenes. Therefore, the book version runs 175 pages.

Special thanks for the kind help, advice and your time, which I know is precious: Mark Feuerstein, Forbes Riley, Aaron Sorkin, The Undeletables (especially Larry, Elisa and KC) Michael J. Weithorn, Ken Cuthbertson, and my family and friends, especially the ones I've never met.

To read more books by bestselling Amazon author Heather Grace Stewart, please visit her official website,

More Books by Heather Grace Stewart:

Strangely, Incredibly Good
Remarkably Great
The Ticket
Good Nights
Lauren from Last Night
The Groovy Granny
Where the Butterflies Go
Leap
Three Spaces
Caged: New and Selected Poems
Stargazing

EXT-MANHATTAN SKYLINE FROM JERSEY CITY
HIGHWAY/INT-FAMILY VAN-DAY

A large family van is stuck in traffic. The
view of Manhattan is beautiful; the inside of
the car, messy and chaotic.

Summer afternoon light streams through the car
windows, casting light on driver JESSICA
(Jess) JANE PAGE-BOULDER, 35. Her face is
beautiful, but worn. She glances in the
rearview mirror at her girls, LILY, 3 and
ELLA, 6. The girls are fighting over a Pokemon
trading card. 'Girls Just Wanna Have Fun'
plays on the radio, along with movie credits.

INT-VAN - DAY

JESSICA is looking in the rear-view mirror. We
see in that mirror a glamorous RICH WOMAN, 28
in a Mercedes Benz. She looks like a movie
star. Successful. Her car MUSIC is cooler,
hipper, younger!

She drives past and glares at Jessica for
going too slow. The RICH WOMAN gives JESSICA
the finger.

Jessica looks disgusted at the woman, but then
looks wearily at herself in the mirror. She
looks back at her kids fighting and throwing
toys around. The van pulls into the driveway.

EXT-JESSICA AND BRIAN BOULDER'S HOME-DAY

JESSICA gets out of the car slowly; she looks

exhausted. She goes to the back of the van, slides the door open, reaches for one seatbelt, starts to get her 3-year-old daughter, LILY, out of her car seat. She pauses for a minute, looks at her, wipes a sweaty hair off her forehead, kisses her tenderly, then continues to get her out of the seat.

                    JESSICA
Okay monkey doodles, we're here. Time to wake
                      up.

Her eldest, ELLA, stretches, looks around, gets herself out of her shoulder strap and joins her mother on the driveway. JESSICA puts down her youngest and goes to grab the groceries in the back of the van, as the two girls run ahead up a stone walkway to the house. Mix through bay window to interior shot.

We follow all three of them now from behind through to a bright, modern family room, where the girls run to several boxes of dress up clothes.

INT-MESSY FAMILY ROOM-DAY

                GIRLS IN UNISON
  (Running to their marmalade cat to pat him)
Princess Sammy Cat! Princess Sammy Cat! We're
hoooome!

                    JESSICA
Good luck, Sammy.

INT-KITCHEN-DAY

JESSICA walks past the girls to a brightly
lit, modern white kitchen. It looks like a
tornado has hit it: dishes line the counter
and the floor is scattered with toys. She
pushes away some dishes and puts down the
groceries on the counter, puts both elements
on, with some rice in boiling water in one pot
and veggies in a steamer in another. She goes
to the kitchen table, opens her laptop and
starts to sit down.

                    JESSICA
        (Calling to the girls as she sits down)
I'm just checking my email girls, back in a
sec.

The girls are giggling in the background, and
'Girls Just Wanna Have Fun' continues again,
louder.

                    JESSICA
Girls, are you still playing nicely?

INT-FAMILY ROOM-DAY

                GIRLS IN UNISON
                You bet Mommy!

They pick up their marmalade cat and swing him
around. He's now in a tutu and costume jewelry
necklaces. They stuff him in a baby stroller
and start spinning him around as they continue
to dance to an increasingly loud 'Girls Just
Wanna Have Fun.'

INT-KITCHEN-DAY

JESSICA sits back and sips that morning's
coffee, makes a face, puts it aside. She looks

terrible. She's in a jogging suit, no makeup.
Her hair is tangled.

                    JESSICA
Kay, Jess, don't stop writing now, the girls
are happy, you're on a roll. Alright. Okay.
This is good.

She prints it off and reads one section aloud:

                    JESSICA (CONT')
She wanted more out of her quiet, suburban
life. She wanted to be more. She wanted
someone to notice her, not as a Mommy, but as
a woman.

Tears well up in JESSICA's eyes, she is
wistful for a moment. Then then her expression
turns to frustration.

                    JESSICA
                This is crap.

She crumples it, tosses the sheet aside,
mumbles.

                    JESSICA (CONT')
                Total crap!

She runs her hands through her hair and keeps
staring at the screen. ELLA enters the room
and runs up to her, right beside her. She
waves her hand across JESSICA's face to get
her out of her writing zone.

                    JESSICA (CONT')
Oh!

                    ELLA

                   Mommy! Earth to Mommmyyyyyy!

                             JESSICA
                   (Still staring at the screen)
          What honey. What?

                             ELLA
          Lily's blue.

                             JESSICA
          Huh? Your sister's sad?

                             ELLA
          No. She's blue. She colored herself
          with my Crayola markers.

          LILY appears from behind her chair, completely
          blue.

                             LILY
          Uh Oh, I blue.

                             JESSICA
          Oh crap!

                             LILY
          Cwap. Cwap!

          JESSICA's coffee spills all over the laptop
          keyboard as she gets up to try to catch her
          daughter, who's begun to run away. Her husband
          BRIAN BOULDER, 40, enters, a loose tie around
          his neck. He has sweat stains from the heat
          and looks unhappy. LILY runs to hide behind
          another chair at the table, but ELLA runs to
          his open arms.

                             ELLA
          Daddy!

                              BRIAN
Ella!

He lovingly sweeps her up and twirls her
around a few times.

He notices Lily hiding behind the chair, but
doesn't get to her yet---first he notices
JESSICA and the coffee. JESSICA is rushing to
soak it up. With Ella in one hand, he holds up
a very wet keyboard with the other hand.

                         BRIAN (cont'd)
How many times have I told you never to put
drinks by the keyboard, Jessica. Now it's
toast.

                             JESSICA
Oops.

                              BRIAN
Are you writing while cooking again? It smells
like someone torched a Chinese restaurant down
there.

                             JESSICA
Oh no! The rice and steamed veggies!

JESSICA quickly gets up to check the stove.

                              ELLA
                    (Whispers to his ear)
                 And Daddy, Lily is BLUE.

LILY runs from the table out of the room.

                             JESSICA

Damn! I can't cook worth shit!

She tosses the sticky burnt rice mess from the pot into the garbage. BRIAN comes up behind her and puts down ELLA, who wanders to the fridge to do fridge magnet dolls. BRIAN gently puts his hands on his wife's shoulders.

                    BRIAN
    You cook great, you just need to pay more
                  attention.

JESSICA twirls around fast and looks at him, tears in her eyes, clearly offended.

                   JESSICA
What kind of back handed compliment is that? You know I'm trying to balance a gazillion things at once.

BRIAN sweeps a loose strand of hair off her face and looks at her softly, like he's about to apologize, but they are interrupted by someone coming into the kitchen. A boy, AIDAN, 9, enters from the side door in a soccer uniform.

                    AIDAN
          (Looks out the door and waves)
Bye guys! Thanks!

                   JESSICA
Hey, how was soccer?

JESSICA backs away from her husband deliberately and goes to the freezer to take out a pizza.

                    AIDAN

Okay.

AIDAN looks at what's left of the burnt rice
in the pot on the stove and rolls his eyes.

                    AIDAN (cont'd)
Burnt rice again?

                    JESSICA
Enough. If you stop with the attitude, we'll
have pizza instead.

                    ELLA
                    Yahoo!

                    JESSICA
Go get changed and washed for supper, and can
you please go wash Lily for me?

                    AIDAN
Where is she?

                    JESSICA
She's hiding up in my office. Ella can help
you.

                    AIDAN
    (Turns, lowers his voice to speak to Ella.)
          What color is she this time?

                    ELLA
She's blue!

                    AIDAN
Cool.

The kids leave the room in a hurry. It's quiet
for a minute as BRIAN leans back against the

counter and JESSICA turns to face him, leaning
against the fridge. She takes the pizza and
tosses it on the counter. They're both tense.

                    BRIAN
We can order out.

                    JESSICA
You know we can't afford to.

She starts to cry but she doesn't come close
to him. There is a visible distance between
them.

                    BRIAN
Who cares, it looks like you've had a long
day.

                    JESSICA
You don't think I'm any good at this. You
don't think I can be both an author and a
Mommy.

                    BRIAN
I didn't say that. I just thought I'd make it
easier tonight.

         INT-AROUND THE BOULDER HOUSE-DAY

JESSICA starts to walk around the house
picking up toys. She starts in the brightly
lit family room that's attached to the
kitchen. BRIAN tries to keep up pace and picks
up a few toys along with her, but he's not as
determined to clean like she is. While picking
up toys and conversing, they walk out of the
family room, down a hallway, into the dining
room, down the hallway again to a more formal
living room, also scattered with toys, and

eventually back down the hallway to the
kitchen.

                    JESSICA
You don't understand what it's like for me. I
was an associate editor, and I was damn good
at it...

                    BRIAN
But you wanted--

                    JESSICA
I know, I know, I wanted more than a few weeks
with the girls. My choice.

                    BRIAN
The right choice.

                    JESSICA
Most days, I think that. Most days. But when
I'm wiping bums and noses all day, I feel
like... Nothing. This big.

She holds up her fingers to show the size of
an insect.

                 JESSICA (CONT')
Oh, you don't get it.

                    BRIAN
Oh sure, make me the bad guy. The guy who
doesn't get you. I work hard, then I come
home, bathe the girls, help Aidan with
homework...

                    JESSICA
You know that's not what I meant.

                    BRIAN

I have no clue what you meant.

                    JESSICA
You can't get what it's like to be a stay at
home mom. It feels like nobody values this job
anymore.

        BRIAN rolls his eyes.

                    BRIAN
Uh-huh. Tell you what.

                    JESSICA
What?

                    BRIAN
Let's switch jobs. You go to the office and
I'll play with Lily all day, then I'll know
how it feels.
And I bet I'll love it.

                    JESSICA
I can't believe you just said that. You make
it sound like the easiest job in the world!

                    BRIAN
I don't think it's easy, but you get to sit
back and have coffee with your sister, and -

                    JESSICA
OK now you're just being an uninformed
asshole.

She throws down a toy, her face full of rage,
but then takes a breath, and her chin starts
to wobble from holding back the tears. Brian
stops picking up toys and looks right into her
eyes.

                    BRIAN
                   (Softer)
I know it's not easy Jess.

                    JESSICA
I'm losing myself. I need more than this.

                    BRIAN
You want to go back to work?

                    JESSICA
I didn't say that.

                    BRIAN
Well then what do you want?

                    JESSICA
I want to be more.

                    BRIAN
More? More what?

                    JESSICA
Just...more. I'm trying to write this novel,
but it feels next to impossible with the kids
hanging off of me from 7 to 7.

                    BRIAN
I can watch them in the mornings, before work.
I've done it before.

                    JESSICA
Sure, but even when I finish stuff, I can't
seem to get it published. I need an agent.

                    BRIAN
God. Not this again.

                    JESSICA
Oh that's nice. Thanks for the open mind.

                    BRIAN
I told you I can't take you on as a client.
I'm new there.

                    JESSICA
You can't or you won't?

                    BRIAN
Don't be like that. It's a conflict; you're my
wife.

                    JESSICA
And you won't help your wife out?

                    BRIAN
I can't help you the way you want me to. I can
help you other ways.

                    JESSICA
Sure, like keeping me barefoot, pregnant, in
the kitchen.

                    BRIAN
Now you're just being stupid.

                    JESSICA
Stupid? Stupid? You know what? There's this
guy on Youtube who can kick himself in the
head 25 times in one minute.

                    BRIAN
He kicks himself in the head?

                         JESSICA
25 times. In the head.

                         BRIAN
                         So?

                         JESSICA
So. Give the guy a call. Learn how to do that.

                         BRIAN
Nice. Real nice. What are you, three? I think
you dropped your soother.

                         JESSICA
Brian, let's calm down...

INT-KITCHEN-DAY
As they return from their circle around the
house to the kitchen, BRIAN's cell phone goes
off at the same time that the kids all run
into the room, chanting, fists in air.

                         KIDS
PIZZA PIZZA PIZZA!

                         BRIAN
Hang on, Jess, I have to take this call.

JESSICA's face falls in disappointment. She
turns and ushers the kids out of the room.

                         JESSICA
Shhhh!

EXT-JESSICA AND BRIAN'S BEDROOM-NIGHT

BRIAN enters a modern bedroom--the walls are
painted deep red and the lights are low. He
gets into bed and looks over at JESSICA, tries

to awaken her to apologize. His expression is
soft and gentle, but she doesn't see it --
she's pretending to be asleep. BRIAN turns off
the light and they go to sleep, their backs to
one another.

INT-KITCHEN-DAY

JESSICA is unkempt in a white, coffee stained
bathrobe. She sits beside JENNY PAGE, 40, a
beautiful but tired-looking woman with similar
features to JESSICA. She's dressed in an
expensive business suit. They're drinking
coffee. BRIAN enters in a hurry. He bends to
give JESSICA a rushed peck on the lips.

                    BRIAN
Kay, I'm late for the meeting, have a good
day.

                    JESSICA
              (forces a smile)
Bye!

BRIAN leaves.

                    JENNY
God, that's exactly how Steve kissed me before
he asked for the divorce.

                    JESSICA
Jenny, don't say that, it's just a rough
patch. Could you play the supportive sister
today?

                    JENNY
I am being supportive. I'm also being
truthful. Is everything okay with you two?

                    JESSICA
It's been better. You remember what it's like
with kids under five.

INT-BOULDER KITCHEN-DAY

                    JENNY
Sadly, Steve and I never figured that one out.
Before we knew it, the boys were 9 and 10, and
we still hadn't agreed how to brush their
teeth. (beat) Shared custody
did us wonders.

Both are quiet for a second.

                    JESSICA
You make light of it all the time, but I don't
know how you survived this last year.

                    JENNY
It's okay. The kids are happier. I'm happier.
I wish I hadn't mated with an ass monkey. You
live and learn.

                    JESSICA
You should have used I-NEED-A-GOOD-MAN.COM.

                    JENNY
Don't joke, I bet it exists.

JESSICA starts fidgeting, looking through some
mail on the kitchen table. She picks up an
envelope and reads the return address.

                    JESSICA
Oh no.

                    JENNY
What?

                    JESSICA
It's from Random House. They've had my novel
for like four months.

                    JENNY
So maybe no word is good word. Open it.

JESSICA opens the letter.

                    JESSICA
Dear Ms. Page, thank you for submitting "No
Ordinary Days". While we enjoyed the read, the
novel doesn't fit with our publishing program

at this time. This is no reflection on the
quality of your writing, blah blah blah,
Bullshit, bullshit, bullshit.

                    JENNY
So it's another rejection. So they don't know
talent. Move on.

                    JESSICA
It's my seventeenth rejection. I'm not sure I
can take any more.

                    JENNY
OK then, Jess, quit. And then what will you
tell your kids?

JESSICA
I know I tell them not to quit. This is
different.

                    JENNY
How?

                    JESSICA
It's not Little League Jenny. It's big time,
big kid dreams, and there's more at stake. I
want it so badly. But maybe I'm just not good
enough.

                    JENNY
Shut up, you are good enough.

                    JESSICA
Well thanks, I think.

                    JENNY
There's only one difference between kids
dreaming of being something great and 40-
somethings dreaming of being something great.

                    JESSICA
Hey I'm not forty yet, speak for yourself,
Cougar.

She turns to a laundry basket beside the table
and begins folding laundry. She throws some
boxer shorts at her sister.

                    JENNY
Shush. Where was I? The difference is the kids
haven't heard "You Suck!" as much as we have.

JENNY starts helping her sister fold,
beginning with the boxers.

                    JESSICA
Huh. That's true.

                    JENNY
And you know where that "You Suck!" voice
comes from?

                    JESSICA
I don't know but I'm pretty sure you're going
to tell me.

                    JENNY
It comes from every single so-called friend,
teacher or boss who made you feel inferior.
Who knows why. Maybe they saw something in you
they wish they had in themselves. But, for
every one of those dimwits, I know you can
think of someone who believed in you.

                    JESSICA
Yes, I can.

                    JENNY
So don't listen to that You Suck voice. Send
the manuscript somewhere else. Keep sending it
till you're 85 with blue hair.

                    JESSICA
I'm never going to have blue hair. Shoot me if
I ever have blue hair.

                    JENNY
Done.

                    JESSICA
Ok, I'll keep sending it out.

                    JENNY
Finally, some logic.

                    JESSICA
Actually, I've started working on this new
novel. I could use some writing time. Could
you drive the kids to school on your way to
the work?

                    JENNY
Say no more. I'll take Lily to the park for a
bit.

                    JESSICA
What about work?

                    JENNY
I don't have to be in court until this
afternoon. Mom's picking the boys up from
school...

                    JESSICA
Perfect! You really think I can do this?

                          JENNY
I know you can do this. It's just a matter of
when. So get writing. No Facebook. No Twitter.
I see everything.

JESSICA picks up the laundry basket, now
filled with folded clothes, and laughs as she
walks up the stairs towards her office.

                         JESSICA
Big Sister is watching huh?

                          JENNY
You bet your blueberry-stained ass I am.

JESSICA looks at the back of her robe. It's
stained blue.

                         JESSICA
Damn! I want sexy back! Or a shower, just give
me back
enough time for a freaking shower!

JENNY laughs. JESSICA puts the basket down and
collapses in defeat on the stairs, shaking her
head and laughing along with her sister.

      INT-JESSICA AND BRIAN'S HOME-NIGHT

JESSICA checks on the girls in their pink,
princess-themed bedroom, then closes the door,
leaving it ajar. She walks up to the master
bedroom where BRIAN is in bed on his laptop
catching up on office work. She stands in the
doorway for a few seconds but he doesn't look
up. She sighs and walks through a dark hallway
to her own office, turning on the light.

         INT-JESSICA'S OFFICE-NIGHT

JESSICA's office is decorated with her two
degrees on the wall and many family
photographs. She's sitting at a large desk in
the corner, and the only light coming from the
room is from her laptop computer. There's a
modern, brown leather sofa against the wall
under a large window. JESSICA is rubbing her
eyes, fatigued, and clearly struggling with
her writing. AIDAN enters.

                    AIDAN
Mom, I can't sleep. I've been thinking. I
shouldn't have dissed your cooking.

                   JESSICA
Oh, Aidan, come over here, honey, it's not a
big deal.

AIDAN walks over and gives her a hug.

                JESSICA (CONT')
You know what? I can't cook. You're right.

                    AIDAN
I'm going to buy you a crock pot when I have
enough allowance saved.

                   JESSICA
That's sweet, but you'd better save your
allowance. You'll be all grown up and taking
out girls before I know it.

                    AIDAN
I will?

                   JESSICA
You will. And girls are expensive. Trust me, I
know.

                         AIDAN
ICK. I don't like any girls. They message me
all the time and I don't know what to write. I
freeze up in front of the screen.

                        JESSICA
                (Looks at her manuscript on
                       her screen)
I know the feeling.

AIDAN sits on her lap.

                     AIDAN (CONT')
                 Watchya writing?

                        JESSICA
Not much. A story about motherhood. It's not
working out.

The manuscript is open on her desktop, as is
her Facebook page.

                         AIDAN
Hey look, one of your friends joined Jack
Venture's fan group.

                        JESSICA
Yea, it's popular.

                         AIDAN
He actually chats with his fans about making
movies? Cool!

He looks at a fan forum with 20,000 members:
Jack Venture's Hollywood Talk.

                        JESSICA

I doubt it's him, he's a big shot actor and a producer. How would he find the time to do that?

                    AIDAN
You should check it out. Maybe it would give you an idea for your book.

                    JESSICA
I don't know about that, but now I just think you're stalling your bedtime. Back to bed! I love you.

                    AIDAN
Love you too Mom.

She looks at a photo of him as a toddler on her desk as she whispers:

                    JESSICA
To infinity!

                    AIDAN
              (Leaving, turns around and
                    smirks)
And beyond!

An upbeat song about friendship and/or getting to know strangers starts to play.

JESSICA looks at Jack Venture's discussion group on Facebook. She hesitates, then presses JOIN. She starts reading the thousands of posts to Jack Venture and finds herself grinning and nodding.

INT-STARBUCKS IN L.A.-NIGHT

JASMINE, a 30-something, professional looking

woman, well-dressed in a grey business skirt and white blouse that shows off her cleavage just slightly is typing furiously on a laptop; a big grin forming on her face as she types. She has a croissant and a latte beside the laptop.

                    JASMINE
Jack Venture, you're biased. It seems to me you're only answering questions from the women with cleavage. Why is that?

                    JACK (V/O)
I can't ignore them. Perfect breasts are like speed bumps in cyberspace.

As the woman reads the answer on her screen, she's shocked at first, but then she laughs out loud.

INT-JESSICA'S OFFICE-NIGHT

JESSICA is reading more posts and laughing out loud. She's happily surprised.

                    JESSICA
Ha! These people are funny. I could waste a lot of time here.

Mix through the office wall to a hospital room. The music changes to a melancholy tune.

INT-JERSEY CITY HOSPITAL ROOM-NIGHT

FRANK WALKLEY, 45, large build, beard/stubble, sad eyes, is sitting on a chair in his wife's dimly lit hospital room. He types to Jack Venture on his laptop:

FRANK (V/O)

Jack, we've almost made it to 25 years, and
during that time, we've watched all your
movies together. I don't know if she hears me,
but when I sit with her, I do some of your
lines for her, just in case she can. Thanks,
Frank.

FRANK gets up from his chair, sets his laptop
aside and goes to sit on the bed beside his
wife, who's hooked up to a respirator, clearly
not responsive. There's a pamphlet on the side
table, 'What You Need To Know About
Withdrawing Life Support.' He takes his
wife's hand and just stares at her, looking
quite lost. The music fades out.

INT-JESSICA'S OFFICE-NIGHT

JESSICA catches her breath. She's moved. She
continues to read the posts.

INT-20-SOMETHING CASTING DIRECTOR'S APT.,
N.Y.-NIGHT

ALEXIS(Alex) ROBERTS is standing looking out
the window. She's a stunning woman, and the
youngest of the group, at 28. She texts a
question in to her cell phone, posting it to
the discussion group.

ALEXIS (V/O)

Jack, what would a date with you be like?

ALEXIS waits a moment, then starts to read
Jack's response on the discussion group on the
screen on her phone.

                    JACK (V/O)
Well, Alexis, I like to show my dates around
my movie sets, then treat them to a quiet
dinner back at my home, and if I'm lucky, the
view of LA from my rooftop hot tub.

ALEXIS sighs a little, stares at her phone
absent-mindedly, and starts to mutter out
loud.

                    ALEXIS
God that's so romantic. No wonder you were
voted the Sexiest Man Alive.

INT-JACK'S BEDROOM, L.A. MANSION-NIGHT

JACK Venture, 30, is sitting on a King size
bed, legs stretched out, wearing only navy
socks. With holes in the toes. And a laptop
covering his crotch. Only his face is tanned,
the rest of his body is stark white. Beside
him we see PEOPLE magazine and his face on the
cover with the headline, Sexiest Man Alive!

EXT-20-SOMETHING CASTING DIRECTOR'S APT., N.Y-
NIGHT

Mix through the apartment window to ALEXIS's
face looking out at NY and then at her cell
phone, smiling gently at JACK's response.

INT-20-SOMETHING'S APT., N.Y.-NIGHT

ALEXIS turns away from the window. Her
BOYFRIEND, a muscular, good-looking, 20-
something, grabs her and closes her cell
phone. He pushes her to the sofa. She looks
uncomfortable as he fondles her, takes off her
T-shirt and unbuckles her bra. He's

unemotional, forceful. After a few minutes she calls out.

                    ALEXIS
Just stop!

She pushes him off her, hastily puts her T shirt but not her bra on, starts to leave.

                    BOYFRIEND
Come on, Alex, you want the part, you know what it takes!

                    ALEXIS
I don't want the part. Not like this.

EXT-20-SOMETHING'S APT. N.Y.-NIGHT

ALEXIS rushes out of the apartment, accompanying music growing louder, working with her every step. Bra in hand, purse in other, she doesn't look back, and doesn't bother with the elevators. She runs down the stairwell. Angry at herself, angry at the world. It's like she's running from every bad relationship she's ever had. The music moves with her from frantic beats back to FRANK's melancholy tune. ALEXIS reaches the ground floor and catches her breath, leaning against a heavy door, with a heavy heart.

INT-JERSEY CITY HOSPITAL-NIGHT

FRANK bends down to his unresponsive wife, kisses her ever so softly on the lips, and gets up to leave the room for the night. He stops at the doorway.

                    FRANK

Goodnight, sweetheart. See you tomorrow.

He turns out the light.

EXT-STREETS OF NY-NIGHT

ALEXIS is tired now. She goes from running to
walking aimlessly alone in the dark, barefoot,
heels in hands with one heel broken, bra
stuffed inside her purse, partly hanging out.
Her mascara's running from the tears. She sits
in Central Park on a bench under a streetlamp,
cell phone in hand. She has read the evening's
responses to JACK's date description and now
types.

                    ALEXIS (V/O)
All the movies make it seem like there are
lots of good guys left out there, but I don't
buy it. I'm done believing. -Alex

INT-JESSICA'S HOME OFFICE-NIGHT

JESSICA reads ALEXIS's post, takes a deep
breath, and frowns. She posts one more
sentence on the group, in reply to ALEXIS. She
talks out loud as she types.

                    JESSICA
Alex, hang in there. Everyday love isn't like
the movies. But sometimes, if we're lucky, we
get movie moments. You have to believe.

                    JESSICA
          (she whispers to herself as
            she logs off Facebook)
...and so do I.

She sits back, looks at her computer, then

starts typing in her manuscript that's
titled...UNTITLED. She's moved and inspired.

EXT-NY CENTRAL PARK ON A FULL MOON-NIGHT
ALEXIS is sitting alone, staring at her cell
phone, looking up at the stars and the
fireflies gathering around a lamplight.

                    JESSICA (V/O)
She misses perfumed postcards, snail mail
letters; conversations in cafés without the
words, "hang on, I have to get this call." She
misses eye contact: knowing gazes and flirty
glances that overpower the urge to send an SMS
or answer the sound of someone somewhere
logging into chat. She texts and types, Tweets
and Skypes, then sleeps outside where stars
and fireflies decorate the infinite darkness.

EXT-NY CENTRAL PARK ON A FULL MOON-NIGHT

The night sky is a blanket of stars and a full
moon, looking down on ALEXIS; alone on a bench
in the vast darkness. The remainder of the
song about strangers becoming friends plays
out, tying it all together.

INT-BOULDER KITCHEN-DAY

Afternoon sun makes the dust bunnies on the
kitchen floor more visible. A high pile of
unwashed dishes sits on the kitchen counter,
right above the dishwasher. JENNY and JESSICA
are making sandwiches for themselves. Lily's
eating Kraft dinner in her booster seat at the
table--and happily making a colossal mess,
covering herself in Ketchup as she tries to
feed herself.

                              JENNY
So what's this new novel about?

                             JESSICA
It's about being a woman. About being a
mother. But so far it's just another ordinary
day. I have no story yet.

                              JENNY
Maybe you need to give the novel a break.

                             JESSICA
And write what?

                              JENNY
I dunno. You could go back to writing
features. How about a review of Jack Venture's
latest movie?

                             JESSICA
Yea, it was good. I love writing about movies.
I used to do that a lot.

                              JENNY
So do it again. Post it on your blog, try to
sell it online. It would do wonders for your
self-esteem.

                             JESSICA
A pair of Jimmy Choo's would probably do more.

                              JENNY
I think a simple shower would probably do
more.

                             JESSICA
                        (sniffs armpit)

Come on it's not that bad.

                    JENNY
Hey, whatever works for you.

                    JESSICA
But I don't know how other mothers figure out
          how to fit everything in.

                    JENNY
I don't think we ever figure that out.

                    JESSICA
Yea.

                    JENNY
And just when we finally get our acts
together, our clothes clean and our homes
impeccable, the grandkids come to terrorize
us.

Jessica laughs and nods in agreement.

                    JESSICA
Can you stay a bit?

                    JENNY
Sure, show me this discussion group I've heard
so much about.

JENNY walks over to the kitchen table, opens
her sister's laptop, and sits down. JESSICA
goes to wipe up LILY's face, playing with her
a little. She tickles her and gives her
zerbert kisses on her neck, then hands her a
cookie.

                    JESSICA
Okay, but I'm warning you, it's highly

addictive.

                    JENNY
Like chips, right? You can't post just one
post?

                    JESSICA
Almost. Almost that bad.

                    JENNY
What draws you in?

                    JESSICA
You wouldn't believe the characters on there.
They have me opening up.

                    JENNY
About the movies?

                    JESSICA
It's not really about Jack's movies. Or any
movies. It's officially about that, but
everyone gets off topic.

                    JENNY
How off topic?

JESSICA walks over to her sister now and pulls
up a chair.

                    JESSICA
Everything from baseball to porn.

                    JENNY
Oh, this I've got to see.

                    JESSICA

Somehow, they make you spill your guts, in
public.

                    JENNY
Wow, usually it takes you at least two Cosmos
to spill your guts.

                    JESSICA
I'm serious. The other night, we were talking
about what we could stand to live without, sex
or coffee.

                    JENNY
Let me guess. The women wanted their mocca
double expressos for life.

                    JESSICA
Pretty much.

                    JENNY
This sounds like a great party. I want an
invite.

                    JESSICA
It's better than a party.

                    JENNY
Yea?

                    JESSICA
Absolutely. You can show up in PJ's., and no
one knows.

                    JENNY
I'm so in. Open the laptop. Now!

They open her laptop and start reading posts
on the forum.

                    JENNY (cont'd)
Oh, there are pictures too? Wow!

                    JESSICA
Yeah, he's posted a few from his movies.

                    JENNY
God look at him. He even sits sexy.

                    JESSICA
I adore that smile.

                    JENNY
He's so sophisticated. So smooth.

                     LILY
          (finishing up her cookie)
YUMMY!

JENNY and JESSICA crack up. They turn the
laptop so LILY can see it better, and then all
three become completely engrossed with what's
on the screen. An upbeat song with great
rhythm starts to play, tying in this last
section.

JESSICA'S OFFICE-DAY

Early morning sunlight streams through the
window. JESSICA is alone in her office, typing
slowly, hesitantly; looking up to the ceiling,
searching for words and inspiration that isn't
coming. She stops to take a sip of coffee from
the mug beside the laptop; sighs, tussles her
hair in frustration, then quickly switches
windows to her Facebook page and opens the
chat feature. She notices ALEXIS's name and
types a chat message to her.

JESSICA V/O
Hey, Alexis. No one seems to be on the group
page. Can you chat?

ALEXIS's name pops up on the screen right
under the words Jessica has typed.

                    ALEXIS V/O
You bet! Come on. I'm always up for
procrastinating.

Jessica's so thrilled to see her friend, she
talks out loud as she types.

                    JESSICA
Hey! How are you?

ALEXIS'S BEDROOM-DAY

FX: ALEXIS is sitting at a computer desk in
her grey, dimly lit bedroom, facing a wall,
full coffee mug in hand. The wall behind her
laptop starts to look like static on a TV
screen. Suddenly, it begins to look
transparent. Within seconds it goes from
static, to transparent, to gone.

INT-PRIVATE CHAT ROOM

ALEXIS and JESSICA are seated opposite each
other on two of three white sofas arranged in
a tight, cosy-looking circle. The room looks
like a café. There are coffee mugs on small
tables to the sides of the sofas. A small
arrangement of gerbera flowers sits in a vase
on the glass coffee table in front of them.
They have their laptops on their laps. The
room has a warm feeling to it. It's lit with

an orangish-reddish glow, but there is no
door, and there are no windows anywhere. The
walls and floors are all black; the furniture
is all white.
They look into each others' eyes and smile.

                    ALEXIS
I've been better. I screwed up another
audition last night. Seriously, I just wanna
give up.

                    JESSICA
You can't do that.

                    ALEXIS
I know, I know, but I feel like it. How's the
novel?

                    JESSICA
Awful. I can't get into the right headspace.

                    ALEXIS
Aw. You know, it's about time we met in
person. You're just a ferry ride away.

                    JESSICA
Today? I have groceries to get, and laundry,
and there's this thing I'm writing...

                    ALEXIS
That's too bad. When was the last time you got
out of the house?

                    JESSICA
Well, um,...

                    ALEXIS
Not to run errands or drive your kids
somewhere, but to do something just for you?

                    JESSICA
Feels like forever ago. But we'll have to
settle for online chat today.

                    ALEXIS
Okay, I have nowhere to be. I have no life.

                    JESSICA
It couldn't have been that bad.

                    ALEXIS
Well, I flubbed half the lines. God I so want
to be good at this! I want to be more than the
girl who's done one commercial.

                    JESSICA
I know how you feel.

                    ALEXIS
You do? But you have a career. You have
bylines out there.

                    JESSICA
Stale bylines. I want to be more than the
woman who did one great magazine piece, and
picks up her husband's underwear off the
floor.

                    JESSICA
What is it about men and underwear?

                    JESSICA
I don't know. There must be some strange force
field around the hamper, making it physically
impossible for anyone but the women to move
in.

                    ALEXIS
I lived with a boyfriend who did that, and I
actually waited a whole week before I said or
did anything. I didn't pick up a single pair
of underwear.

                    JESSICA
And? It worked?

                    ALEXIS
By Sunday there were seven boxers in a pile on
the floor, one foot from the hamper.

                    JESSICA
It's a conspiracy. They're getting us back for
the PMS, I just know it.

FX: The new friends sit back and laugh, and as
they do so, their laptops slowly vanish from
their laps.

                    JESSICA
So, the audition...was it nerves?

                    ALEXIS
I think so.

                    JESSICA
So you just need to do more auditions.

                    ALEXIS
I've been auditioning for two years solid.
Commercials, TV, movies, everything.

                    JESSICA
Oh. No bites?

                    ALEXIS
I landed that one commercial.

                    JESSICA
That's good then. Do I know it?

                    ALEXIS
PAL Dog food. The dog stole the scene. I'm
hoping it only shows in foreign countries.

JESSICA laughs.

                ALEXIS (cont'd)
It's just that I quit my job so I could have
more time for auditions.

                    JESSICA
What did you do before?

                    ALEXIS
I taught Bakrim yoga.

                    JESSICA
Bakrim?

                    ALEXIS
Yes it's this hot yoga. Fire yoga, in a very
warm room. I wasn't very good at that, either.

                    JESSICA
No?

ALEXIS
I fainted a couple times. The class didn't
know what to do with me.

                    JESSICA
Really.

                    ALEXIS
They had to carry me out on a stretcher. I
actually frightened students away.

JESSICA puts down her coffee on the side table
beside her and can't help herself. She has a
hearty laugh. ALEXIS joins in.

                    JESSICA
In your defense, I don't get why people would
want to bend their bodies like pretzels inside
a toaster oven.

                    ALEXIS
Right? I just want to be good at *Something*.
I think acting is it, I really do Jessica,
but--

                    JESSICA
Okay, if you're an actress, be an actress.
Play a new character every day.

                    ALEXIS
Every day?

                    JESSICA
Every day. Like, if you were in a diner right
now, you could ask the waiter for something.
But you could do it as...

                    ALEXIS
As..?

                    JESSICA
As Marilyn Monroe.

                    ALEXIS
Oh no. No, I'm not any good at her.

                    JESSICA
Try. You should try.

                    ALEXIS
I don't know. Maybe. Maybe someday. (beat)
Hey, thanks for believing in me.

                    JESSICA
Thanks for the chat--but I guess I should get
some writing done now.

                    ALEXIS
Kay, bye!

FX: The walls become transparent, then static,
then solid again.

INT-ALEXIS'S NY APARTMENT-DAY
ALEXIS is back in her bedroom, logging off her
laptop at her desk.

INT-JESSICA'S HOME OFFICE-DAY
Jessica is seated at her desk. She changes
windows from Facebook to the window with the
manuscript for her novel, and types in a
section called NOTES and writes the phrases
"Bakrim yoga--pretzel, toaster oven" and
"Special force field around the hamper." She

rereads these words and starts to grin.

An upbeat song plays as she gets back to work.

INT-LILY AND ELLA'S BEDROOM-NIGHT

The girls are in their twin beds. JESSICA has just tucked them in. She walks over to the door and stands in the doorway, about to turn off the light.

> JESSICA
Goodnight girls. Love you.

> ELLA
Mommy do the song!

> JESSICA
Sure, sweetie. "You are my sunshines, my only sunshines, you make me happy, when skies are grey, you'll never know dears,

LILY AND ELLA
> How much I love you!

> JESSICA
Please don't take my sunshines away.

LILY and ELLA grin and snuggle into bed more.

> ELLA
Mommy?

> JESSICA
Yes honey.

> ELLA
Mommy, no one can ever take your sunshine away, because it's so, so very high up in the

sky!

                    JESSICA
You know what, you're right. You're so right.

                    ELLA
I know.

                    JESSICA
Goodnight El. Goodnight Lily. Sleep tight.

                    GIRLS
OK!

JESSICA turns off the light, leaves the door
ajar a little and walks away.

        INT-JESSICA AND BRIAN'S BEDROOM- NIGHT

JESSICA climbs into bed beside BRIAN. She has
a notepad and pen on her lap. He has his
laptop and a lot of paperwork around him, and
is absorbed in his work.

                    JESSICA
So, they're asleep.

                    BRIAN
No shenanigans?

                    JESSICA
Not yet.

                    BRIAN
Great.

                    JESSICA

I'm working on a new novel. Alex loves my
ideas.

BRIAN finally looks up.

                    BRIAN
Alex from that discussion page?

                    JESSICA
Yes. We chat online a lot. I'd like to go meet
her in Manhattan soon.

                    BRIAN
You really think that's a good idea? What
about Lily? She could be some..some..I don't
know...

                    JESSICA
What, some aspiring actress who kidnaps me and
demands I clean her house and do her laundry?
Come on, Brian.

                    BRIAN
No, I'm just saying, it's a little weird
becoming friends with someone you've only met
online.

                    JESSICA
Brian, most people today don't even stop to
tell you the time. These people tell me their
hopes and fears, and they make me laugh. I
like them.

                    BRIAN
But they're friends you've never met. Isn't
that an oxymoron?

                    JESSICA

Nope. It's just contradictory. An oxymoron has
to combine two contradictory terms.

                    BRIAN
Smart-ass English major. So, like, online
friends?

                    JESSICA
Or loving husband.

                    BRIAN
Be nice now.

                    JESSICA
Maybe I've never met them, but they're better
for me than you are sometimes.

Brian sits up more and moves his body farther
away from his
wife.

                    BRIAN
Go have an orgy with your online friends then,
Jess, if they're all you need to be happy.
Just go.

                    JESSICA
Brian, I didn't mean it like that. (beat) But
I think what I need to make me happier is you
taking me on
as your client.

BRIAN lets out a long frustrated sigh.

                    BRIAN
We've been through this before Jess. I can't
take you on as a client. What would my

colleagues think?

                    JESSICA
Yes, what would they think. You, helping your
wife, dreadful.

                    BRIAN
Stop. Just stop. Besides, I already have my
plate full with the clients I have.

                    JESSICA
No room for your best friend then.

                    BRIAN
Jess, don't say that. This is business.

                    JESSICA
Maybe if you read it, you'd change your mind.

                    BRIAN
             (Holds up other manuscripts)
I'm doing too much overtime as it is. Do you
want me to be your husband or your agent? I
can't be both.

                    JESSICA
What you're being is completely unfair. Let's
just stop, the kids are going to hear us.

BRIAN gets up out of bed, picks up his papers.

                    BRIAN
Fine!

He storms out of the room.

JESSICA watches him leave and calls out after
him.

                    JESSICA
Fine!

Melancholy music plays as JESSICA lies down,
grabs her
pillow, and starts sobbing into it.

INT-BOULDER KITCHEN-NIGHT

BRIAN grabs a beer from the fridge. He's
mumbling angrily to himself. He starts
rummaging through the kitchen cupboards and
the fridge looking for something to eat. As he
realizes he can't find what he wants, he slams
the beer down and foam comes pouring out of
it.

                    BRIAN
Damnit!

BRIAN doesn't attempt to clean the mess up. He
leans against the counter, takes a deep
breath, and puts his hands in his head,
rubbing his eyes. As he does so, he notices a
photo of Jessica and him on the fridge.
They're standing beside the ocean, kissing
each other. It looks like it was taken on
their honeymoon. He grabs the beer, shakes off
some of the wetness, then sighs, and raises it
up to the photograph.

                 BRIAN (cont'd)
You two are a couple of knuckle heads, you
know that? The honeymoon, it doesn't last. And
the for better or worse part? Some days, it
feels like it's never gonna get better.

He takes a swig of the beer.

                    BRIAN (cont'd)
And I'm not sure there's anything I can do
about that.

He sighs, and speaks in a near whisper now.

                    BRIAN (CONT')
I don't know what I can do.

The melancholy music plays out as BRIAN keeps
drinking his
beer, staring glumly at the photos on the
fridge.

INT-JESSICA'S OFFICE/JENNY'S KITCHEN /ALEXIS'S
APT/ FRANK'S LIVING ROOM SOFA-DAY

Mid-day sunlight streams through JESSICA's
office window. She's on her laptop, and we see
JENNY and FRANK are also with her online on
the discussion page.

FX: At first, everyone is at their laptops on
their desks or on their laps, but within
moments these computers melt away, and the
walls that separated them go from solid to
static to transparent to no walls--to the
black walls and revolving glass door of the
public discussion room.

INT-ONLINE, PUBLIC DISCUSSION ROOM

This café-like room looks like the private
chat room, only it's larger, and it has a
brightly lit, large, revolving glass door at
the back of the room. There's a warmly-lit
coffee bar in the corner of the room and
behind it a woman, MODERATOR, wearing all-
white, is serving three people different types

of fancy coffees. 10 LURKERS--people of all
walks of life--come in and out of the large
glass revolving door and sit in white chairs
farther back from the sofas. From time to
time, they glance at the main group that's
talking or go to the bar to order a drink, but
they don't ever jump into the conversation.
The group sits in a cosy circle of modern
white sofas and easy chairs, looking into each
others' eyes. ALEXIS enters through the
revolving glass door and comes to sit down
beside FRANK.

                    FRANK
Hey! What's up?

                    ALEXIS
Another date gone terribly wrong. I think I'll
just become a nun.

                    FRANK
Don't do it, Alex. Please. What a waste!

FX: Everyone's laptops vanish from sight.

ALEXIS laughs along with FRANK. JESSICA sits
back, looks at ALEXIS, takes her hands in
hers.

                    JESSICA
Alex, come on, you're gorgeous. And talented.
You need to believe in yourself more.

                    ALEXIS
I know. I've just chosen all these selfish
users.

                    FRANK

Losers?

                    ALEXIS
That too. My last boyfriend was a real winner.
When I tried to find out where we stood, he
told me "It is what it is."

                    JENNY
He said "It is what it is?"

                    ALEXIS
That's what he said.

                    JENNY
What does that even mean?

                    ALEXIS
I have no clue, I thought you might know.

                    JESSICA
We might need the urban dictionary.

                    ALEXIS
Oh but they'll just tell you it's a cross
between "Suck it Up." And "Que Sera Sera." Not
what he actually meant by it.

                    JENNY
And you didn't ask him what he meant?

                    ALEXIS
Well, it was obviously the brush off. He wrote
it in a text message.

                    FRANK
Ouch. He may as well have asked, do you want
fries with that?

                    ALEXIS

(laughing)
It's just as pointless, but at least then I'd
have gotten fries!

                    JENNY
I think you need an older guy.

                    ALEXIS
You think?

                    JESSICA
Not much older. Just not 20 something. Someone
who knows who he is.

                    ALEXIS
Someone like Jack Venture?

                    JESSICA
Oh, he knows who he is, alright, but do we
know for sure it's really him who's chatting
with us here?

                    JENNY
Oh, come on Jess, it's gotta be him. We've
been chatting with him here for months. They'd
have shut it down by now if it was phony.

                    JESSICA
I dunno. I want to believe, but then my
journalistic instinct kicks in, and...

                    FRANK
You overthink things. What we need to do is
figure out how to call his studio. We'll call
and confirm.

                    JESSICA
I guess we could Google it. Hang on. I'll log
off and go try.

JESSICA gets up off the sofa and goes through the revolving
door.

INT-JESSICA'S HOME OFFICE-DAY

Jessica is at her laptop. She's searching Google for listings for Jack Venture, producer. She finds a name and starts typing a post to the others into the Discussion forum:

We see these words on the screen:

                    JESSICA (V.O)
I found it. I'm going to call now.

She picks up a phone and starts to dial.

                    JESSICA
I can't believe I'm doing this.

INT - JACK'S MOVIE STUDIO- L.A. OFFICE-DAY

A young woman, KIMBERLY, mid-20s, is sitting at a desk in an office, with busy people walking around her. She answers the phone.

                    KIMBERLY
Kimberly Fife.

INT-JESSICA'S HOME OFFICE-DAY

                    JESSICA
Ms. Fife? Um. JESSICA Page, I'm a journalist in Jersey, um, looking for um, Jack Venture?

                    KIMBERLY (V.O.)
Yes, this is Jack's personal assistant

Kimberly.

                    JESSICA
    Um, I'm on the Facebook forum and I'm just
          wondering, is that really him?

                    KIMBERLY
Yes, it is. He does interact with his fans
there.

                    JESSICA
Oh, so with all the calls from the press
you're getting about this fan page now, you're
probably going to
kill him.

INT - JACK'S MOVIE STUDIO -L.A. OFFICE-DAY

JACK walks in, piles a bunch of mail on
Kimberly's desk, grins, and gives her a goofy
thumbs up sign. He has his iPhone on his left
hip in a brown leather hip holster, and
earbuds in his ears; he's engrossed in his
favorite tunes. He does a few hip gyrations
and starts doing the moon walk from her desk
to his office. He's fun, in a geeky way. He
trips at the very end of his moonwalk,
collects himself, waves at Kimberly, enters
his office a little embarrassed. He's
adorable, but far from the Sexiest Man Alive.

                    KIMBERLY
               (trying to contain her
                    laughter)

Oh yea, I'm going to kill him
alright.

                    JESSICA (V.O)

(laughs)
Okay, thanks for the confirmation.

INT-ONLINE DISCUSSION ROOM

JESSICA returns to the group's cozy café
through the revolving door and sits back down
at her place on the white sofa. ALEXIS, FRANK
and JENNY have been deep in conversation, but
as she arrives they all lean in towards
JESSICA in anticipation.

                    ALEXIS
So, it's him then?

                    JESSICA
Sounds like it. Jack Venture's actually
chatting with us online!

The two giggle like teenagers. FRANK and JENNY
just smile at each other. They all sit back,
relaxed.

                    FRANK
I read he's going to be interviewed by Evelyn
Powers today.

                    JESSICA
Seriously? Oh I have to go again then guys, I
really want to see this.

                    ALEXIS
Okay, meet here tonight then?

                    FRANK
TV sucks lately. Sounds good.

All of them quickly get up to "log off" the
discussion page. JESSICA is the first to leave

through the revolving doors, with the others
trailing behind her. An upbeat song plays out.

INT-THE EVELYN POWERS SHOW SET-DAY

A flat TV screen shows the words "Taped
Previously." JACK walks out looking gorgeous.
Pure sophistication. He does a little dance to
the music before sitting down. It's smooth.
EVELYN POWERS, 40, a petite, blonde, energetic
woman, gives him Hollywood-style kisses and a
hug.

                    EVELYN
Jack, charming as always!

Jack unbuttons his suit jacket and gets
comfortable.

                    JACK
Thanks Evelyn. I feel the same way about you,
but I guess I don't stand a chance.

                    EVELYN
No, but Mama's real interested.

The audience laughs and claps.

                    EVELYN
Seriously. You're single, aren't you?

JACK
You've been reading People magazine haven't
you? According to them, I'm too busy making
movies and jet-setting around the world.

                    EVELYN
Isn't that why?

                         JACK
                         Nah.

He looks a little uncomfortable. He hesitates,
then grins out at the audience

                      JACK (CONT')
I just haven't found the right girl yet.

                        EVELYN
That's so sweet!

The women in the audience are swooning. Some
hoot and
whistle, others applaud.

INT-EVELYN POWERS SHOW SET-DAY

EVELYN POWERS and JACK VENTURE are fully
clothed but standing together in a shower, in
shower caps, for EVELYN's Bathroom Series.
They sing something current and popular.
EVELYN can't sing but throughout the song she
improvises, showing off some great comic
timing, and along with her, JACK's goofball
humor shines, too.

EXT-BUSY TELEVISION STORE-DAY

ALEXIS is standing on a busy NY street,
looking through a large store window, chatting
on her cell phone with someone, while watching
the end of the Evelyn Powers show on one of
several TVs on sale in the window. She can't
stop laughing as EVELYN finishes off the song
on a very wonky high note. The show goes to
commercial.

                    ALEXIS
Wasn't that great?

                    JESSICA (V.O)
Oh God, I haven't laughed that hard since my
doctor asked if I wanted to try natural
childbirth.

                    ALEXIS
Don't know about that, don't want to. Okay,
I'm going to try to get him chatting with us
on the page more. I'll post a new question.

                    JESSICA (V.O)
Cool, I'll watch for it, bye!

ALEXIS leans against the store window, and
brings up the latest group posts on her cell
phone. She types in a question.

                    ALEXIS (V/0)
Jack how fit do you have to be for your roles?

INT-JACK VENTURE'S OFFICE-DAY

JACK has his feet up on his desk. He's been
tossing a Nerf basketball into a basket on the
wall, but not getting it in.

He looks over at his laptop and notices some
new posts in the forum, including ALEXIS's new
post. He goes to type his response.

                    JACK
            (typing and speaking slowly,
                to get it right)
Well, Alexis, I do like to keep in shape.

INT-JACK'S PRIVATE GYM-DAY

JACK is on a rock climbing wall in his home.
He's got a trainer yelling at him like he's a
complete loser. JACK is struggling, big time.
But he's laughing at himself. The Spiderman
Theme by Michael Bublé--Big Band version--
plays.

                    JACK (V.O)
I'm training hard for my next role. I'm doing
all my own stunts. It's coming along...just
great... so
far.

JACK is trying to climb but doing more
bouncing around in the harness. He's a
complete klutz. Pathetic. After some time
hanging tangled upside down, he moves to the
treadmill. His trainer yells at him like he's
an army cadet. He's so fatigued he trips and
bonks his head on the controls. The whole
thing falls apart, and both his body and the
machine come tumbling to the floor. There's
some great physical comedy here while the
Spiderman Theme plays out.

INT-JESSICA AND BRIAN'S BEDROOM-NIGHT

Jessica is in a bathrobe in bed, typing on her
laptop. Brian enters in his pajamas. He stands
above the bed a moment, waiting for her to
stop typing. She looks up at him, her
expression sad and distant. He gets into bed,
but she doesn't move. He looks at her a
moment. She finally stops typing.

                    JESS
What?

                    BRIAN
So...I guess I should learn more about these
online freaks...er...friends of yours.

                    JESS
That's not funny.

She lets out a deep breath and starts to type
again.

                    BRIAN
    Jess, let me be part of this. Please. Don't
                shut me out.

                    JESSICA
You aren't letting me in your literary world,
why should I let you into this one?

                    BRIAN
Come on. I'm trying here.

                    JESSICA
They aren't freaks. We're good friends now.
You have to stop making fun of this.

                    BRIAN
Ok. Who's the guy? Should I be worried?

JESSICA's expression softens. She laughs a
little.

                    JESSICA
Frank? God no. He's like a big brother. We
talk about photography, and sometimes he
spills about his situation.

                    BRIAN
Situation?

                    JESSICA
His wife has been in a coma for six months.
She kept getting infections after her surgery.
She can't breathe on her own. She's not
getting better.

                    BRIAN
God, that's awful. I can't imagine.

                    JESSICA
We shouldn't waste our time fighting.

                    BRIAN
I agree. How bout this. I'll read your novel
half way through. I'll help you polish it, if
you want.

JESSICA bites her lip and looks down at her
laptop.

                    JESSICA
Yeah, that would be okay, I guess.

BRIAN
Good.

BRIAN opens up his briefcase, and JESSICA
reopens her laptop. Their bodies remain
distant from one another. Each looks at the
other for a moment when the other isn't
looking. Sad music plays.

INT-JESSICA'S OFFICE/JENNY'S KITCHEN /ALEXIS'S
APT/ FRANK'S LIVING ROOM SOFA/VENTURE'S
BEDROOM-NIGHT

JESSICA, JENNY, FRANK, ALEXIS and JACK are all
online on the discussion page, typing away on
their laptops.

FX: At first we see their laptops on their desks or on their laps, but within moments the walls melt away, just as they did before.

INT-ONLINE, PUBLIC DISCUSSION ROOM

The group is sitting down in a now-familiar circle of modern, white sofas. They have laptops on their laps, but they look in one another's eyes, enjoying a regular conversation.

                    FRANK
You have to appreciate what you've got. I don't think I told her enough, and now she can't hear me. And now I have to let her go.

                    JENNY
She can hear you Frank. She can hear you.

FRANK starts to cry. He grabs a tissue.

                    FRANK
Would someone please lighten things up in here? I'm being such a downer.

                    JESSICA
You're only a downer if you see yourself as a downer.

                    JENNY
OK, I'll do what I can to lighten things up here, but I can't promise very much after we were just Dr. Phil'd to death by my younger sister.

                    JESSICA

Are you challenging me here? Because, trust me, I know how to lighten things up. Are you ready for this?

ALEXIS reads this, grins, puts her hand up to her mouth.

                    JESSICA (cont'd)
Sex in the movies. Why is it that people
always carefully tie up bathrobes afterward? I
mean, really, who puts on a bathrobe after
they've been naked with someone?

                    ALEXIS
I know!

FX: As everyone laughs, their laptops simply
vanish.

                    JENNY
Actually, I wear one. I don't want anyone
staring at my big arse as I waddle to the
bathroom.

JACK walks through the revolving glass door at
the back of the room.

                    JACK
Big arse? Did someone say big arse? That's my
cue to log in.

                    JESSICA
And who has a long chat with their lover
afterward?

JACK flops down on a sofa beside ALEXIS.

                    ALEXIS
Hey Jack!

                    FRANK

(laughs)

Yes that one's a little silly. It's obviously
a technique to establish character. This
character usually just cuddles and falls
asleep.

JACK

Jessica, I'm a little confused. I thought you
ladies wanted the chat. We men are real tired
after sex. We do the chat because we think
it's what you want. Now you're telling us it's
not what you want?

JESSICA

Maybe I'm not the norm, but no, I don't want
the chat. I work hard during sex, too. I want
the snuggle. And the "That was Amazing." And
the ice cream, after we've had a rest. But no,
I don't want the chat.

ALEXIS

I agree. I figure, if the guy has enough
energy to chat me up after, he didn't do his
job right.

FRANK
(laughs)

You ladies are harsh tonight!

JESSICA

No, we're telling it like it is. You hate when
we play games. This is what women want. Are
you guys paying attention?

JACK

Paying attention? Hell, I just called my
assistant in here to take notes.

Everyone laughs. A catchy tune plays out over

the group enjoying a relaxed conversation.

INT-JESSICA AND BRIAN'S BEDROOM-NIGHT

Softer, sexier music plays. BRIAN is looking
over some manuscripts on the bed. JESSICA is
in a negligee beside him, reading a novel but
not really paying attention to it. She's
trying to get him to notice what she's
wearing. Soft, sexy music plays on their clock
radio.

                    BRIAN
Damn, gassing up the new car is costing us a
bundle.

                    JESSICA
Can't you stop thinking about stuff like that
for once?

                    BRIAN
Would you just relax? I have to think about
stuff like that, Jess. We have a family I'm
responsible for. I can't always be Mr. fun
guy.

                         JESSICA
Don't tell me to relax!

                         BRIAN
Don't be a nag.

                         JESSICA
I could still get Mr. Fun Guy you know. JACK
Venture notices me. He actually flirted with
me today.

                         BRIAN
          (he doesn't look up from his bills)
So go be with Jack Venture then.

                         JESSICA
Fuck you! I just want you to pay more
attention to me.

                         BRIAN
          (looks up, a little shell shocked)
Well I'm here aren't I?

    He takes off his reading glasses and looks
                  right at her.

                    BRIAN (CONT')
I'm right here beside you. And this morning I
tried -

                         JESSICA
This morning I had kids to get ready for
school, the cat puked on the stairs, and I got
my period. Forgive me if my Samantha Jones
side wasn't exactly shining.

BRIAN can't help but laugh. He tries again.

                    BRIAN
You don't think I notice you? I do, Jess.
Every day. Every single day.

                    JESSICA
                   (softens)
You should show me more often.

                    BRIAN
Maybe I'm not the-what is it? - Hottest Man
Alive like Jack Venture. Maybe we never get
the chance to say more than two words in
private anymore, but...

He starts to play with the delicate straps of
her negligee -but abruptly stops when AIDAN
enters the room. The soft sexy music abruptly
stops as well.

                    AIDAN
Mom! Dad! Ella says I'm a Poo-Poo Head, and
Lily won't stop grabbing at my iPad. I want a
room in the basement!

                    ELLA
You ARE a Poo-Poo Head!

LILY walks in with an ipod on and AIDAN's
underwear on her head.

                    LILY
POOPY HEAD, POOPY HEAD!

                    AIDAN
Hey give me those!

JESSICA and BRIAN give each other a look of
longing.

JESSICA looks like she's going to cry. BRIAN
sighs and gets up from the bed.

                    BRIAN
I'll go. I'll go. Come on everyone, back to
bed.

A beautiful melody that conjures up feelings
about the challenges in relationships begins.
BRIAN goes to put the kids all back to bed.
JESSICA watches the family walk out of their
bedroom and sighs. She looks at their wedding
photo beside the bed and tears well in her
eyes as she lies there and then falls asleep
with the picture beside her, and the song
playing out.

EXT-BOULDER FAMILY BACKYARD-DAY

The sky is a brilliant blue. Songbirds call
out from the large oak tree in the center of
the yard. Early morning sunlight shines on
JESSICA's contented face as she walks out the
back door to a small table on their patio.
JESSICA smells the air, sips her coffee, opens
her laptop. When she opens an email from
FRANK, her peaceful expression turns to
sadness for her friend.

INT-JERSEY CITY HOSPITAL ROOM-NIGHT

Sad music plays with footage of FRANK standing
beside a hospital bed while the doctors are
discontinuing ventilator support on his wife.
Every move of his body shows that he can't
take just standing there while this happens.
He gets onto the bed and holds her, like
they're spooning in bed at night, as she dies.
He's holding onto his best friend for dear

life as if that will bring her back.

INT-FRANK'S BEDROOM-DAY

A small ray of early morning light falls on
FRANK's bed. FRANK stands in the shadows. The
light falls on his hands as he clings to his
wife's pillow, staring at the empty space
where his wife used to lie. He finally exits
the room.

INT-FRANK'S LIVING ROOM SOFA-DAY

Frank walks to the living room sofa, blanket
in hand, in an attempt to sleep there instead.
He tries to get comfortable, but tosses and
turns.

                    FRANK (V.0)
God has her now, and I want her back. I want
her back! Since she's been sick, I've always
kept to my side of the bed. I always made sure
to leave room for her. For when she came back.
She was supposed to come back! The thought
that I no longer have to do that
is...intolerable...

EXT-BOULDER BACKYARD-DAY

JESSICA wipes tears running down to her nose.
She keeps reading the email.

INT-FRANK'S BEDROOM-DAY

FRANK makes up the bed, then messes it up,
throwing the pillows and sheets and blankets
around everywhere in a fit of rage and grief.
He falls to the floor.

                    FRANK (V.O.)
I've made it through the first night without
her, but I don't know how to make it through
the rest. All those nights. I just don't know
how.

The sad music plays out here to end this scene
with footage of FRANK struggling with the bed,
and his emotions.

EXT-BOULDER BACKYARD-DAY

JESSICA is on her cell phone. She's upset.

                    JESSICA
Frank? It's Jess. I got your email.

INT-JERSEY CITY FLORIST SHOP-DAY

FRANK in on his cell phone, standing in front
of some roses.

A female FLORIST, 40, is beside him, helping
him pick out flowers for the funeral.

                    FRANK
I can't believe you're calling.

                    JESSICA
Of course I'm calling. I couldn't text my
condolences.

                    FRANK
You'd be surprised. You're my first phone
call.

JESSICA is taken aback with that comment on
society.

                    JESSICA
Wow. Huh. It's a whole new world. How are you
holding up?

                    FRANK
I've been better.

                    JESSICA
My Mom can watch the kids. I'm coming to the
funeral. It's time you became a friend I've
met. Oh, Jenny's coming with me.

                    FRANK
                  (laughs)
Sure, bring along the older sis, in case I'm
some weirdo.

                    JESSICA
Listen weirdo, she wants to meet you too. And
Alexis emailed me, she's coming in from
Manhattan sometime this afternoon.

                    FRANK
Things are looking up Jess. Thanks so much.

                    JESSICA
You bet. And Frank?

                    FRANK
              (visibly choked up)
Yes pipsqueak?

                    JESSICA
Everyone's going to tell you to be strong. But
you don't have to be strong.

                    FRANK
No?

                    JESSICA
No. You be whatever you need to be.

EXT-BOULDER HOME DRIVEWAY-DAY

BRIAN is holding LILY in his arms; JESSICA's
MOM, 60, is farther up the driveway occupying
AIDAN and ELLA with a game of basketball. He
gives his wife a quick kiss on the lips as she
gets into JENNY's car. JENNY is in the
driver's seat.

                    BRIAN
Don't worry. Between the two of us we have it
covered.

                    JESSICA
You don't think this is weird?

BRIAN
There are stranger things. I met you on a ski
lift.

                    JESSICA
Yea that ski mask should have been my first
warning.

                    BRIAN
You're with Jenny, and you'll stay in Jersey.
It's fine.

                    JESSICA
Are you saying you were wrong about the online
thing?

                    BRIAN
I'm saying sometimes you have to take the
leap,

                    JESSICA
and figure out how to pull the parachute on
the way down.

                    BRIAN
You remember. What I said about us.

                    JESSICA
How could I forget. You were in a ski mask.

                    BRIAN
It was cold! And the 80s.

They kiss through the car window. JENNY rolls
her eyes. The kiss is brief, a little forced,
and interrupted by the kids who come to kiss
JESSICA through the window too, and JESSICA
and JENNY's mother as well.

                    MOM
Take care of each other.

                    BRIAN
Call me so I know you're safe.

                    JESSICA
I will.

                    MOM
          (chasing kids down driveway,
calls, waves as car pulls out)
Be safe, girls!

EXT-JERSEY CITY FUNERAL HOME-DAY

ALEXIS is standing outside the funeral home.
JESSICA goes to greet ALEXIS by extending her
hand, but then she pulls her in for a hug.
ALEXIS shakes hands with JENNY, then JENNY

pulls her in for a hug. The three ladies walk
inside
together.

INT-JERSEY CITY FUNERAL HOME-DAY
Soft, sad music plays behind JESSICA's voice
over.

                    JESSICA (V/O)
Life is fragile, and so is love. We think it,
say it all the time tell each other we're
going to spend more time together, less time
at work/paying bills/reading other people's
Facebook profiles. Drive slower, eat better,
love longer, because you never know what
tomorrow will bring.

INT-JERSEY CITY FUNERAL HOME-DAY

People file in and sit down. Time passes as
the funeral proceeds, with FRANK doing a
reading, then JESSICA standing up and doing a
reading. Family and friends are present, but
there is visible space around FRANK on the pew
where he sits. Until JESSICA, JENNY and ALEXIS
scoot over and sit closer to him.

EXT-JERSEY CITY FUNERAL HOME-DAY

The coffin is taken out of the funeral home.
FRANK walks in the pouring rain to the hearse.
Others follow him through the pouring rain to
their cars.

                    JESSICA (V/O)
But life gets in the way, and we're back to
the races. Not enough hours in the day to call
an old friend, let alone digest our food,
savor our wine, say 'I love you' first. Life

is fragile, and so is love.

EXT-JERSEY CITY HIGHWAY-DAY

The same shot of Manhattan from the opening
scene, but this time it's gray and somber. The
procession proceeds along the highway to a
graveyard.

EXT-JERSEY CITY GRAVEYARD-DAY

Everyone stands around the coffin, umbrellas
in the rain. FRANK falls to his knees as the
coffin is lowered.

                    JESSICA (V/O)
Of course, you will forget this in about five
minutes. Your boss will start yelling at you
or your toddler will pee on the floor or your
phone bill will arrive and you'll wonder why,
God damn it, you got double billed again.
You will forget about the fragile parts and go
on surviving.

EXT-FRANK'S LIVING ROOM-DAY

FRANK's living room is full of people--mostly
elderly aunt types; very conservative people.
They're all standing around eating sandwiches.
It's noisy, crowded, hot. FRANK is in a corner
alone. JENNY, JESSICA, and ALEXIS walk up to
him. He puts down his plate and turns to
JESSICA.

                    FRANK
Remember when you told me to be whatever I
need to be?

                    JESSICA

Yes.

FRANK
I've decided what I need to be is drunk.

JESSICA
Okay then. Drunk it is.

ALEXIS
Anything you need Frank.

All three ladies look at each other. JENNY
heads toward a table with liquor bottles on it
to fix him a drink.

FRANK
No, let's go out the side door. I need to
leave. It's like somebody died in here.

JESSICA and the girls look at each other
again, shocked at first, but then they start
to smile. They follow his lead out the door.
No one even notices they've left.

EXT-FERRY TO MANHATTAN-DAY

A rousing, upbeat song plays. FRANK, JENNY,
ALEXIS and JESSICA are in their black/dark
funeral attire on the ferry from Jersey to
Manhattan, looking out at the water and the
sun as it sets--stunning. They chat
incessantly. They are an unlikely group of
friends, varying ages and shapes and sizes,
but it works. They really listen to each
other. They look into each other's eyes. They
laugh a lot. They have chemistry.

INT-NY PUB-NIGHT

It's a cozy Irish pub and the atmosphere is
upbeat and lively - total contrast to FRANK's
somber living room. JENNY is up at the bar
getting another pitcher of beer. ALEXIS,
JESSICA and FRANK are sitting at a table,
quite relaxed.

                    JESSICA
So you think they've noticed you're gone yet?

                    FRANK
Doubt it.

                    ALEXIS
They won't hold this against you?

                    FRANK
Sure they will, but I don't care. It's mostly
just her uncles; a couple old aunts.

                    JESSICA
So you're avoiding an evening of kissing men
and women with mustaches. Good thinking.

                    FRANK
I never got along with them anyway. They
didn't like that we never had kids.

                              ALEXIS
Can I ask why you never had kids?

                              FRANK
Sure. It's not that we don't like them. I mean
I'm a cub scout leader. I love kids.

                             JESSICA
Of COURSE he's a cub scout leader.

                              ALEXIS
Of course. I wish you didn't feel like my
brother. You might be the perfect man.

                         FRANK laughs.

                              FRANK
Thanks doll! Yea, we talked about kids, but
then Jean and I started the business together,
and we got occupied with working. It just
slipped us by. By the time we wanted a baby,
we were too old.

                             JESSICA
You would have made an excellent father.

                              FRANK
Thanks. And thanks for this, ladies.

FRANK raises his glass.

                         FRANK (CONT')
I've always wanted siblings. Now I've gained
two kid sisters --online, of all things.

JENNY comes up to the table with a pitcher of
beer.

                         JENNY
So what does that make me, then, the old hag?

FRANK smirks but doesn't answer. He looks down
at his beer. A beautiful modern melody with an
Irish flute in the background begins to play.
FRANK recognizes as his and his wife Jean's
song.

                         FRANK
Oh that's just great. Murphy's law. that was
our 20th wedding anniversary song. We danced
to that, at our party. She danced with me. We
danced.

                         JENNY
Oh, Frank.

                         FRANK
It's okay. I'm going to be okay.

The music lowers. He looks down at his beer
glass, then looks up again slowly. He is
completely vulnerable.

                      FRANK (cont'd)
Do you think she knows it was me who killed
her?

                         JESSICA
Stop being ridiculous. You didn't kill your
wife. An infection killed her.

                         FRANK
But I made the decision.

                         JENNY
You two made that decision years ago. It's a
decision you hope you never have to act on.

                    JESSICA
But you had to act on it.

                    FRANK
So I did the right thing...

                    ALEXIS
Sweetie, you know you did.

They sit in silence for a few moments,
drinking their beer. FRANK starts smiling just
a little as the anniversary song grows louder.
The other girls are smiling now, too.

                    JESSICA
Come on, we need to eat something
other than tiny sandwiches.

They all agree and stand up to leave. The
beautiful music plays louder as they walk out,
at first a slight distance apart, then,
starting with JESSICA moving toward FRANK,
linking arms, with FRANK in the middle of the
foursome.

EXT-STREETS OF MANHATTAN-NIGHT

They walk out of the pub and down the road
together, arms linked in friendship and
support of FRANK. The song plays out as they
walk, and, the street lamps come on one by one
as they walk along the road.

INT-FANCY NY RESTAURANT-NIGHT

The friends are still in their black /dark
funeral attire, sitting in a restaurant
enjoying a fancy meal--outside. They're

already well into their champagne. It's a
rooftop restaurant at a hotel. There's a pool
to the side of the tables. It's clear as
glass: everyone is eating or mingling around
the pool drinking cocktails, no one is in it.
Everyone is chattering away and laughing, but
JESSICA looks uneasy. She takes her cell phone
out of her purse.

                    JESSICA
Guys, I'm just going to check my messages and
email before dinner gets here.

                    FRANK
You're too much of a geek with that thing.

                    JENNY
Oh stop, you're just jealous because you
barely know how to poke someone on Facebook.

                    FRANK
I do so! But it's stupid and totally-2008, so
I don't.

                    ALEXIS
Go ahead Jess.

The rest of the gang goes back to talking.
JESSICA checks her email on her phone. To her
surprise, she finds a message in her inbox,
from JACK Venture. She keeps this to herself.
The message in her inbox reads: Jack Venture
commented on your blog post.

                    JESSICA (V/O)
He signed my blog. He actually signed my blog!
"Thanks for sharing your blog link with us at
Jack Venture's Hollywood Talk. Great stuff"

JESSICA types back slowly, discreetly, under
the table, after taking a minute to figure out
what she wants to write.

                    JESSICA
Thanks back, so much. Are you for real?

She sends the email. Seconds later, an email
lands in her inbox. We see it's from
You_dont_know_JACK@verizon.com When she looks
up from the table, JACK is standing there, in
a tux, looking gorgeous. He hands her a glass
of champagne.

JESSICA looks around at her friends. Her
friends look over at her and smile--of course
they can't see her imagined, idealized JACK.

She's takes the champagne, but she's flustered
now. She puts her cell phone to sleep in
embarrassment. JACK disappears. She gets up
now from the table and walks to a private
hallway in in the interior part of the
restaurant. She stands there with her back
against the wall, waiters walking past, wakes
up the cell again, and texts.

                    JESSICA (V/O)
I got everyone talking about sex on the group
page. Things got pretty hot. But maybe I
should stop and have you take over.

A few seconds pass, she awaits the response
nervously. Now he's also standing against the
wall, right beside her and he brushes aside
some hair and whispers in her ear.

                    JACK
No, Jess, please, keep doing what you're
doing, exactly how you're doing it.

She giggles and blushes and turns her head
away from him. She quickly closes her cell
phone. When she puts her cell phone to sleep,
JACK disappears.

She feels the heat in her cheeks and her chest
with her hands, then saunters back to her
friends in a dreamlike state.

                  ALEXIS
So I've always wanted to come here, and I
thought this was the perfect reason.

                   FRANK
Hell, yea, but you shouldn't have waited. You
hear me?

He turns around to face other diners.

                FRANK(CONT')
Don't wait people! Don't wait! Tomorrow may
never come!

JENNY laughs, then takes FRANK's champagne
glass, sets it aside, and hands him his fork.

                   JENNY
Okay, Frank, lovely sentiment, but people are
going to start wondering where your cloak and

sign are.

JESSICA is still catching her breath from her
exchange with JACK, but it's barely visible
that she's distracted by it.

                    JESSICA
She's right, Doomsayer Dude, you should eat
something with that champagne.

He complies for a second. Everyone's quietly
eating.

JESSICA stares out at the sereneness of the
pool. Music starts to play. The pool is
beckoning her.

                    FRANK
Alright. You know you wanna.

                    JESSICA
Huh? Wha?

                    FRANK
It's killing you. You've been thinking about
it since we got here, haven't you?

                    JESSICA
Thinking about what?

                    FRANK
I can see it in your eyes. CANON BALL.

                    JESSICA
Oh, is this a challenge?

                    FRANK
It's actually just an observation on my part.

                    JESSICA
And tell me, what have you observed?

                    FRANK
Well, I had some help from my friend Henry
David Thoreau.

                    JESSICA
Thoreau?

                    FRANK
Yea, I like quotes, especially his.

                    ALEXIS
He's drunk, and he's about to quote some guy
who lived in the woods.

                    JENNY
At least it's not Shakespeare. I'd like to get
out of here tonight.

                    JESSICA

What does Thoreau have to do with me jumping
into that pool?

                    FRANK
                  (softly)
Well, he wrote, how vain is it to sit down to
write when you haven't stood up to live?

Time stands still for a second. It's a
challenge. And a life regret, on FRANK's part.
She looks right at him. They look at each
other in silence for a minute. Now there are
tears in her eyes. And now, there are tears in
his eyes.

                    JESSICA
I should smack you, both for the geeky quote
and for insulting me.

                    FRANK
But you're not going to smack me?

                    JESSICA
No, because you're right. You're right. Damn
it Frank, you are fucking brilliant. You
people, you're all fucking brilliant.

                    JENNY
Well I wouldn't exactly call me brilliant, but
something like that, yes.

                    ALEXIS
People call me two sandwiches short of a
picnic, actually.

                    FRANK
Ah, yes, but at least you've got the
champagne.

They all raise their glasses to toast each
other. But as their glasses clink, there are
only three glasses in the air. They turn their
heads to look for JESSICA, and realize she's
running full-force toward the pool in her long
black dress.

                    JENNY
Oh my God. She's really doing it.

                    JESSICA
YEEEE HAAAAAAAWWWWWWWWW!

JESSICA canon balls into the pool without
hesitation. Two good looking waiters rush over
with towels. She gets up, wrings out her long
black dress, and lets the waiters wrap her in
the towels. They don't scold her, they're
laughing, and so is she. People do stare.
JESSICA just grins at them. Then she waves,
bows, and walks over to her ecstatic friends.
She feels so alive. Triumphant, joyful music
plays.

INT-ALEXIS'S NY APARTMENT-DAY

While everyone is goofing around and cooking
breakfast, JESSICA finds a quiet spot alone in
the living room. She is using her cell phone
to talk with BRIAN.

                    JESSICA
So, we're going to stay here at Alex's place
in Manhattan till Sunday. I'm feeling a bit of
Mommy
guilt about that.

INT-A HOTEL ROOM IN JAPAN-NIGHT

BRIAN is sitting on a hotel room bed chatting
on the phone. It's a very small room and the
bed's headboard is up against the wall.

                    BRIAN
Don't, you could use the break.

                    JESSICA (V/O)
First time without them in nine years.

                    BRIAN
Has it been that long?

                    JESSICA (V/O)
It's been that long.

                    BRIAN
I wasn't paying attention.

                    JESSICA (V/O)
No, you weren't.

                    BRIAN
I need to work less.

                    JESSICA (V/O)
How'd you come to realize that?

                    BRIAN
I haven't seen you naked in nine years either.

INT-ALEX'S NY APT-DAY

                    JESSICA
Stop, it hasn't been that long.

                    BRIAN (V/O)
Eight?

JESSICA smirks and changes the subject.

                    JESSICA
So you're there three more nights?

                    BRIAN (V/O)
Yea, Sorry this trip was so last minute. Mom
was more than happy to watch the kids and

INT-A HOTEL ROOM IN JAPAN-NIGHT

He stops mid way through. He senses something
is wrong. He looks around the room.

                    BRIAN
Oh my God, I think we're having an earthquake.

The music changes. Something's not right.

INT-ALEXIS'S APARTMENT-DAY

                    JESSICA
Oh my God. Oh my God. Or maybe it's
terrorists. Hang up! Go! Go for cover.

JESSICA hangs up the phone, then sits there,
staring at it nervously, waiting for it to
ring. After a moment, it rings.

She quickly picks it up.

                    BRIAN (V/O)
I'm back.

                    JESSICA
Oh my God, are you okay?

                    BRIAN (V/O)
You aren't going to believe this.

                    JESSICA
You're okay?

                    BRIAN (V/O)
I'm fine. I was wrong.

                    JESSICA
Wrong?

                    BRIAN
It was the couple in the room next to me.

                    JESSICA
The couple in the room...

          INT-A HOTEL ROOM IN JAPAN-NIGHT

                    BRIAN
The couple in the room next to me. They're
doing the horizontal mambo.

Muffled groaning sounds and foreign (Japanese)
words are coming from the wall behind BRIAN.
His bed is actually shaking a little bit.
BRIAN is laughing so hard he's shaking a
little, too.

INT-ALEXIS'S APARTMENT-DAY

JESSICA laughs hard along with her husband.
Then she realizes what his mistake has just
done to her.

                    JESSICA
Don't you ever scare me like that again!

                    BRIAN (V/O)
Hey, it's sex with subtitles. Honest mistake!

                    JESSICA
You're pathetic.

                    BRIAN (V/O)
I miss you. Maybe we can talk about your
novel...

The line cuts out.

                    JESSICA
Brian? Brian? Brian, can you hear me? Damn it!
                    (softly)
I miss us, too.

INT-NY RESTAURANT-DAY

The gang is sitting back in a family-type
casual dining room, relaxing over a lunch of
chicken and fries. The music in the background
is upbeat.

                    ALEXIS
We can go back to my apartment again after
this. Try on the high heels we got.

                    FRANK
I have dibs on the maroon Naughty Monkeys.

                    JENNY
You need to start hanging out with dudes.

                    FRANK
Not a chance. Are you kidding me? This is
Women Studies 101.

                    ALEXIS
For when you're ready to start dating again?

                         FRANK
Yea, that, too.

                        JESSICA
It's kind of quiet in here. We need to liven
things up. Come on Alex, show time.

                        ALEXIS
No thanks, Jess, I'm saving it all for my next
                       audition.

FRANK turns his head and glances at a table
across the restaurant. The music changes.
Something is off.

INT-NY RESTAURANT-A FEW TABLES OVER-DAY

FRANK notices a lovely looking petite WOMAN,
45, at the other table with her hands around
her neck, panicking. He rushes over from his
table to the other table, grabs the woman from
behind, and performs the Heimlich. A chicken
bone comes flying out of her mouth, and she
passes out in his arms.

The husband, DEAN, 50, a tall man with a bad
haircut, outdated mustache and terrible
fashion sense, isn't paying attention. He and
his family are completely engrossed in their
discussion, totally oblivious to the scene
beside them. When he sees a large man with his
arms around his wife, he thinks FRANK is
attacking her. The minute he sees the wife
limp in FRANK's arms, he jumps up and punches
FRANK in the eye.

                         DEAN
YA BIG CREEP!

Everyone except the husband gasps. It's a hard hit. FRANK falls instantly to the floor, the woman with him. Everyone stands in shock and silence for a few seconds. FRANK is unconscious, and the woman has passed out. No one is tending to her. JESSICA bends down and tries to awaken both of them.

Two waiters come running and stand before FRANK on either side. The husband starts talking to them about the incident.

                    DEAN
I want you to call the police.

JESSICA has managed to gently wake both FRANK and the wife. The wife looks around and realizes what's happening.

                    WOMAN
No no, NO Dean...

She tries to talk but realizing she's nearly lost her voice--it comes out raspy. She holds her throat and continues to speak in a near whisper.

                    WOMAN
You idiot. This man saved my life. I was choking.

                    DEAN
You were choking?

                    WOMAN
For crying out loud, I have to choke for you to notice me anymore?

                         DEAN
No, God no! We were talking about baseball,
and

                         WOMAN
Shut it, and apologize to the man!

                         DEAN
Good God. What do you say. What's that
expression, ha ha, um. my bad? I um, let me
help you up.

He just stands there and forgets to help FRANK
up.

                         WOMAN
My bad? I can't believe you punched him out.

The PUNK ROCK WAITER, 18, bright blue hair,
multiple piercings on his lip, looks down at
the woman.

                    PUNK ROCK WAITER
M'aam, I need to know if you'll be, like,
pressing charges?

                         WOMAN
No, we won't be, like, pressing charges. Does
no one listen any more? He's a hero.

Her family finally stands up, and with
JESSICA's encouragement they help the wife to
her feet. The husband is still just standing
there, dumb struck. The wife looks at him,
then holds out her hand and helps get FRANK to
his
                         feet.

                    WOMAN (cont'd)
Thank you. I can't say it enough.

She extends her hand and he takes it. She
pulls him in for a hug.

                    FRANK
You might want to go to a hospital, check
everything out - you were out for a bit there.

                    WOMAN
Your eye...

                    FRANK
It's okay m'aam. I have another one.

It's like no one else is in the room. She
stands like a statue and just smiles at him,
and he smiles back. Everything is said with
their eyes. After a moment, he turns and walks
out of the restaurant, overcome with emotion.
His friends follow him out.

INT- NY IRISH PUB - NIGHT

The gang is sitting at a table in the same
Irish pub they enjoyed the previous night.
JENNY is up at the bar, getting a pitcher of
beer; looking very attractive in a sexy red
sweater. Two younger, very attractive but very
inebriated guys come up on either side of her.

                    GUY 1
You should be more careful.

                    JENNY
Yeah?

                    GUY 2
Yeah. You shouldn't wear red.

JENNY looks uncomfortable, but she can take
care of herself.

                    JENNY
Why shouldn't I?

                    GUY 1
You see, red attracts bulls.

                    GUY 2
And we're the bulls.

                    JENNY
Yes, you are, and I've had quite enough bull
shit for this year, wankers.

The guys look surprised to be turned down.
JENNY turns, leaving the pitcher of beer
behind, and walks briskly back to her table to
her friends.

                  JESSICA
You okay hun?

                    JENNY
I'll be fine. The boys nearly lost their nuts.
I'll be fine.

                    FRANK
A little too eager huh?

                    JENNY
Like a couple of Shake Weights still in the
box.

                  JESSICA
            (spits out beer with laughter)
Ack!

                    JENNY
I need to get out of here. Somewhere I'm not
reminded of my ex-husband.

                    FRANK
You miss him.

                    JENNY
Are you fucking kidding me?

                    FRANK
Okay, then!

                 FRANK stands up.

                 FRANK (CONT')
And I need to dance this off.

                    JESSICA
You dance? like, in time? To the music?

                    FRANK
I'll have you know I was voted Prom King.

                    ALEXIS
Really?

                    FRANK
Really, not.

                    ALEXIS
Good dancing? I know just the place.

          EXT-COX DANCE CLUB-NY-NIGHT

The group is standing in a long line-up
outside COX bar: a flashy, noisy night club.
They're the stand-outs in the crowd. The
misfits.

                    JESSICA
It's called COX?

                    ALEXIS
You heard it right. Cox. C-o-x.

                    JENNY
  The bar is called Cox. Whatever the cover is,
                I'm paying it.

                    JESSICA
Even if it's a gay bar?

                    JENNY
Especially because it's a gay bar.

                    FRANK
I can't believe I'm doing this. My mother is
rolling over in her grave.

                    ALEXIS
Oh, you'll see. The dancing is great in here!

                        FRANK
I'll bet.

INT-COX DANCE CLUB-NIGHT

The four friends are dancing together, having
a blast. Just being themselves. FEATHER BOA
GAL, 40, a very tall, trans woman in a
platinum blonde wig, heels, fashionable black
cocktail dress, and big pink feather boa
starts dancing with them. She isn't "in drag"
--she identifies with female as her gender and
looks very much like a woman. She's very
friendly, but not flirting, just having fun.
FRANK is quite uneasy at first. The others
start goofing off and being playful with
FEATHER BOA GAL. FRANK is mortified, but
loosens up slowly.

Time passes. Now they're all dancing in a
chorus line to '500 Miles,' The Proclaimers.
All four have formed a chorus line and are
kicking up a storm. FEATHER BOA GAL is in the
middle, pink feather boa flying. When it comes
to the "da da da da" part, they break away
from kicking and face each other. One group
taunts each other with one part, shouting it
at the other group, then the other with the
other. They're loving it.

                  FRANK AND LADIES
I would walk 500 miles and I would walk 500
more just to be the man who walks a thousand
miles to fall down at your door.

            FEATHER BOA GAL AND FRIENDS
DA DA DA DA

                  FRANK AND LADIES

DA DA DA DA

                    FEATHER BOA GAL AND FRIENDS
DA DA DA DA

                         FRANK AND LADIES
DA DA DA DA

                              ALL
DA DA DA DA DA DA DA DA DA DA DA DA
DA!

More time passes. It's the end of the night.
FRANK is sitting on the sticky pub floor, his
back against the wall.

                            FRANK
She was just a beautiful soul, you know? I
just want to share her love with everyone.

The camera moves to reveal who is sitting
beside him. FEATHER BOA GAL is sitting beside
FRANK, sobbing and dabbing her eyes with a
Kleenex. She blows her nose before turning to
FRANK.

                       FEATHER BOA GAL
Honey, I'm so glad you did. What a love story!

EXT-STREETS OF MANHATTAN-NIGHT

The streets are dark, lit only by the odd
street lamp along the way. The song is still
playing as the four walk home with their arms
linked. They're laughing and falling all over
each other. They stop at the crossing light.
FRANK looks at the light, then looks at his
friends. The music fades.

                    FRANK
                  (slurred)
Ladies, pay attention now. There's a little
green man there ... (he points up to the
crossing light)

                  FRANK(CONT')
and he says it's time to go!

He stops a minute, lets go of the ladies, and
spins around underneath an old streetlamp.
Arms wide open, he's turning, turning;
amazingly, not falling. He keeps spinning as
he shouts to anyone and everyone walking by.

                    FRANK
I saved someone's life today. I did the hei,
hei, heim, Well, whatever it's called, I did
it.

                  FRANK (CONT')
I SAVED SOMEONE'S LIFE TODAY!

It's very quiet for a moment as the friends
stand still in near-darkness, watching this
man who's mourning his wife and celebrating
life all at once, spinning around, his arms
open wide to the sky.

After a moment they all crack up laughing,
especially FRANK, and he falls into them. They
catch him. After he regains his balance, they
link arms again and begin crossing the street
together.

INT-ALEXIS'S APARTMENT-DAY

Early morning light streams through ALEXIS's
apartment windows onto the floor. Everyone
except ALEXIS is asleep on the sofas, looking
tired and hung over. ALEXIS is in the
kitchen, looking through several cupboards.
She can't find what she's looking for. She
looks at the clock. 8 a.m. She looks at her
friends a moment, then grabs her jean jacket
off of the coat hook and leaves the apartment.

EXT-ALEXIS'S APARTMENT BUILDING-DAY

The streets are barely busy as the city wakes
up. Birds are singing in the trees; cars and
taxis come to a screechy stop at the lights; a
few people are bustling along the side
streets.

EXT-NEW YORK 50'S STYLE DINER

ALEXIS runs across a street towards a diner's
glass door. The sign on the door reads OPEN.
She walks through the door, a little bell
jingling behind her as she walks through.

INT-NEW YORK 50'S STYLE DINER

The 50's style diner is crammed full of people
having breakfast. The place is cheery and
well-lit, with a black and white checkered
floor and bright red tables and chairs. ALEXIS
knows where she's going. She walks right up to
the counter where a sign reads FRESH BAKED
BAGELS and speaks to a female SERVER in an
apron behind the counter.

                    ALEXIS

Can I have a dozen sesame bagels to go please?

                    SERVER
Sure, but we just put a new batch in the oven,
it'll be about five minutes.

                    ALEXIS
That's fine. I'll pay now.

She hands the SERVER a twenty over the
counter, and the SERVER returns with change
for ALEXIS. As ALEXIS puts the change in her
pocket, she glances around the diner. She
notices a red, glittery chair in the corner
that's placed right in front of a mirror. A
smile slowly creeps across her face. She looks
around at the many people eating breakfast.
She looks back at the chair.

                 ALEXIS (cont'd)
Oh, what the hell.

She smirks as she gets into character. She
waves her hand toward a very good looking
young WAITER, 20.

            ALEXIS (AS MARILYN MONROE)
Excuse me. I'd like to see the menu please.

The waiter smiles and hands her the menu.

                    ALEXIS
What? No diamonds? That's just not acceptable.

She totally goes for it. She jumps up onto the
red chair and starts to sing -and she's
surprisingly good.

                 ALEXIS (SINGS)

A kiss on the hand may be quite
continental/But diamonds are a
girl's best friend/A kiss may be
grand but it won't pay the rental
On your humble flat, or help you at
the automat/Men grow cold as girls
grow old/And we all lose our charms
in the end/But square cut or pear
shaped/These rocks don't lose their
shape/Diamonds are a girl's best
friend.

The WAITER applauds her, along with the rest
of the people in the restaurant who, much to
ALEXIS's surprise, are all grinning. A few are
even whistling. ALEXIS takes a grand bow.

The WAITER helps her down off her chair and
grins. He can't take his eyes off her.

                    WAITER
Trust me when I tell you, that was the
highlight of my day.

ALEXIS remains calm and collected, but smiles
at the WAITER.

                    ALEXIS
Thanks, me too.

He stands there staring and grinning at her
for a moment.

                    WAITER
Okay. Let me know if I there's anything I can
do with, er, do for you.

ALEXIS gets her jacket and her bag of bagels
which are now waiting for her on the counter.

She waves at the SERVER and walks out of the
diner, the little bell on the door ringing
behind her. She turns around and looks at the
diner from the outside, then jumps up and down
for a minute, squealing.

                    ALEXIS
YES! Nailed it.

She stops jumping, composes herself, and walks
back to her apartment with a spring in her
step.

EXT-ALEXIS'S APARTMENT BUILDING-DAY

Afternoon sunlight covers ALEXIS's apartment
building. ALEXIS is waving goodbye to her
friends, who are leaving in JENNY's car. They
hoot and holler out the windows, expressing
their gratitude.

                    ALEXIS
Awesome weekend guys!

                    JESSICA
Meh. It was what it was.

                    ALEXIS
Shut up. And get writing!

INT-JESSICA'S OFFICE-DAY

JESSICA is sitting at her computer. Early
morning sunlight streams through her office
window onto her desk. Her hair is neat and
she's got some makeup on now, but she's in a
baggy t shirt and jogging pants again. The
house is clearly empty--she has time to work
all alone. She types an email.

                    JESSICA (V/O)
Jack, my blog's gotten so many hits since you
commented! Thanks again for the vote of
confidence. Now if I could just get unstuck
with this novel...

A moment later there's an email in her inbox.
JESSICA grins as she reads the email. When she
looks up, JACK is sitting on her desk, legs
crossed, in boxer shorts, an open white robe,
expensive silver watch, with a Men's magazine
in his hand. He looks buff, tanned, delicious.

                       JACK
Jess, you're a very talented writer, and you
shouldn't ever not wear the dress you're
wearing in your profile picture.

JESSICA giggles and hesitates. She actually
looks around for a moment; it's her guilty
conscience. Of course, when she does this,
he's not there. She touches her neck and chest
gently. She's turned on, and she wants to feel
good; to flirt and be witty back. She sits
back in the chair, looks at him with a
mischievous grin.

                     JESSICA
I just noticed the early hour there for you in
L.A. Wow, I could actually be be the first
thing you do in the morning.

JACK puts down his newspaper, leans forward on
the desk, and grins at her.

                       JACK
Absolutely, but I'd take a hot shower first.

She opens her mouth, stands up to do or say
something provocative. There's an intensely
hot moment where their faces are close and
they're both grinning their dirty thoughts at
each other. Then she thinks about the
situation one more second, and he disappears.

                    JESSICA
                   (Typing)
I'm going to go behave now, JACK.

She turns to go and hears a new ping sound -
he's written her a response.

                    JACK (V/O)
Why are women like you always married?

She grins, closes the laptop, and walks away,
grabbing a laundry basket on the stairs and
taking it up to her bedroom.

INT-JESSICA AND BRIAN'S BEDROOM-DAY

She drops the laundry basket on her bed and
catches her reflection in the mirror. She
stops. She stares. She smiles.

She sees herself in a new light. Special.
Sexier. She peels off her t shirt and jogging
pants in a hurry and throws them aside.
They're a hindrance, she has to get rid of
them. She's in lovely purple silk panties and
matching bra. It's completely unexpected how
beautiful her body is under the baggy, dingy
clothes. She looks in the mirror and pushes in
her belly with her hands as she sucks it in.

                    JESSICA

Muffin top.

She turns around a little, looks at her butt, shakes her arms so the flab on the underside starts to wobble.

                    JESSICA (cont'd)
Helloooooo there Cellulite.

Her face falls to a frown.

                    JESSICA (cont'd)
Stop it. You have to stop doing that to yourself.

She pauses, lets her hair down, shakes it, then emphatically tells her own image in the mirror:

                    JESSICA (cont'd)
You. are. a. Sex. Goddess.

JESSICA can't get the insane grin off her face.

                    JESSICA (cont'd)
The first thing he does in the morning.

"Addicted to Love" by Robert Palmer begins to play. She opens a shoe box on the floor beside the mirror. Red Naughty Monkey heels. She slowly, seductively puts them on and admires them for a minute in the mirror. So now she's in sexy underwear and killer heels. She goes to the nearby broom closet and gets out a long-handled floor sweeper (Swiffer type), puts a dust cloth on it, then struts over to

the mirror and absent mindedly sprays perfume
from the back of her ears down to her breasts.
It's like she doesn't even know she's done it.
She does some very sexy dance moves in the
mirror to the music, then kicks off the shoes.

INT-STAIRS-DAY

She prances down the stairs to the beat of the
music with the sweeper in her hands. She's
Swiffering the wood stairs and swinging from
the stair railing, arching her back on the
beats as she lets the railing take her whole
weight. She hangs from the railing a couple
times before running down the stairs and
dancing into the family room.

INT-FAMILY ROOM-DAY

Toys and books litter the floor. JESSICA kicks
them aside, barely bothered. She's far too
into the moment. She uses the leather ottoman
toy box as a stage, jumping up and then
stepping down a few times. She Swiffers the
wood floor a little to the rhythm of the
music, then puts the Swiffer between her legs
and thrusts back and forth to the music. It's
inappropriately hilarious. It's between her
legs, then it's a cane beside her long legs,
then it's being pointed in the air, then it's
thrown to the side and

JESSICA is shaking her booty like a Coyote
Ugly girl. It's unbridled, unpolished, yet,
somehow, sexy.

JESSICA is dancing like no one has ever seen a
Suburban mom dance with a Swiffer before.

The music plays out until just near the end, with JESSICA falling, exhausted, into a leather chair, where she sits with a big silly grin on her face. She is laughing at herself as the song ends.

EXT-BOULDER'S BACKYARD PATIO-DAY

LILY is playing outside with JESSICA'S MOM pushing her on the swingset.

INT-KITCHEN-DAY

JESSICA is glancing out the window at her MOM and LILY and smiling. She's standing at the kitchen counter with her laptop, reading yesterday's emails from JACK--again. She grins, catches her breath and starts to type.

                    JESSICA
Jack, as a married woman, anything I reply to that would have to self-destruct in five minutes. Kind of like how I feel when I'm chatting with you. What's that called again, spontaneous combustion?

                    JACK (V/O)
There are other words for it, but, yes.

JESSICA reads it and laughs out loud. Then she stops and realizes something.

                    JESSICA
Oh. my. God. This is great stuff. This is it. Holy crap, this is it!

She closes the laptop and does a little excited fast dance --throw-down-the football

style--her legs moving very quickly as she
squeals in glee.

INT-STAIRS-DAY
She quickly runs up the stairs with her
laptop, up to her office.

INT-JESSICA'S OFFICE-DAY

JESSICA opens her laptop again, then opens a
Word document. She sits down and deletes the
title: UNTITLED NOVEL. She studies the
discussion page --names of her friends and
their profile photos --which she's also opened
up in a window beside the Word document.

DISSOLVE TO

EXT-NY RESTAURANT-DAY

In slow motion, JESSICA is once again doing a
massive canon ball into the pool, her friends
are looking on laughing, grinning, applauding.

BACK TO

INT-JESSICA'S OFFICE-DAY

JESSICA smiles as she studies the photos of
her children on her desk. On her blank title
page, she writes the words THE FRIENDS I'VE
NEVER MET: A Novel by Jessica Page and then
she starts typing furiously and laughing and
crying and laughing and crying again as she
types. She cannot stop, it's a flood.

Three sentences seen on her computer screen
are:

She jumped into the pool, fully clothed--her
first canon ball since she was five years old.

Somewhere between the air and the water, she found herself again.

"I decided what I need to be is drunk," he said to them.

Spontaneous combustion?

INT-JESSICA'S OFFICE-NIGHT

BRIAN pokes his head into the room. She hears him and turns her head around.

                    JESSICA
Call me butter, cuz I'm on a roll!

BRIAN laughs and walks a little closer to her.

                    BRIAN
That's great, corn on the cob. I'll go burn some rice to go with that.

                    JESSICA
Shut it. Just shut it or I won't share the royalty cheques.

                    BRIAN
Got it. And I've got the kids.

                    JESSICA
Thanks.

She stops typing now and turns her whole body around to look at him.

                    JESSICA (CONT')
Tell the kids I promise to take them to the park tomorrow.

                    BRIAN
I will.

                   JESSICA
You know I love you, but, GO.

BRIAN grins and leaves the office.

INT-JESSICA'S OFFICE-NIGHT

The clock moves forward and the room grows
darker. JESSICA is still typing furiously.

INT-JESSICA'S OFFICE DAY

JESSICA is in the same clothes -she's clearly
worked through the night. She looks tired but
determined, keeps typing, a little teary eyed.
With the voice over, poignant footage plays
out from her life as a wife and mother--
cleaning up piles of toys, brushing little
teeth, holding little hands, kissing away
scrapes and bruises-- as well as footage of
her typing away.

                 (JESSICA V/O)
Perhaps I am a fool to admit what generations
of women before me forgot to mention. Or,
maybe they were too afraid? Most of the time,
being a mother is a blessing. But sometimes,
you just want to run and hide. Pretend you're
Some One Else, Some Where Else. Be alone with
the woman you were before. Try to find her
again among the toys strewn across the family
room floor. Try to forget for a moment that
odd feeling of loneliness despite the loving,
gooey hands forever linked to yours. I love
being your mother. I love your spirits, and
your friendship, and the way you have enlarged

my heart and taught me more about myself than
I ever dreamed possible. But this motherhood
thing, its' a full-time job. Unpaid,
unnerving, often unpleasant. It is a calling.
Only strong spirits need apply.

INT-KITCHEN-DAY

As the V/O plays out, the younger children are
hanging onto their father, grabbing onto his
tie and shirt. AIDAN is just getting in the
way. BRIAN is trying to make several lunches,
but it's not working. The girls start fighting
with AIDAN. BRIAN's expression is one of "What
have I gotten myself into?"

INT-JERSEY CITY PARK-DAY

It's after school. JESSICA, JENNY and their
mother are going for a walk in the park. LILY
is in a stroller; ELLA is running around a
little ahead of her mother. JENNY is dressed
in a pant suit for work. JESSICA is dressed
nicely and looks showered. The walking pace is
quite quick. They're trying to get exercise
and keep up with ELLA ahead of them. They're
walking while talking along a path and the
camera follows both in front of them and
behind them.

                    JESSICA
I can't believe it. Suddenly, I'm writing this
piece of fiction based on my own nutty life.

                    MOM
About what?

                    JESSICA
About motherhood and writing and the charming

yet slightly crazy people I've met on the
discussion page.

                    MOM
How are you managing all this with the kids?

                    JESSICA
Brian's been helping me out lots in the
mornings.

                    MOM
You see, that man is solid to the core.

                    JESSICA
I know that. I do know that. I just wish we
still had the fireworks.

                    MOM
Honey, when you have three children, you're
lucky if you get a spark.

                    JESSICA
That's just it. I want the spark back.

                    MOM
He's a good man - he's not at the bars
drinking or fooling around with other women.
Remember that.

                    JESSICA
I do. I guess sometimes, just sometimes, it's
like, is this all there is?

                    MOM
I know. I think there's a song.

                    JENNY

If there isn't, I'll write it.

                    MOM
You know, I went through all this with your
father, especially when you girls were very
young. It ebbs and flows dear. (quietly)
Imagine, we're 40 years in.

                  JESSICA
And when I asked for your secrets to success,
you weren't exactly helpful.

                   JENNY
Yea remember what she wrote in that book at
your wedding shower?

                 ALL THREE
RUN AND HIIIIIIIIDE!!!

It takes a moment for their laughter to
subside.

                   JENNY
Stop! Stop it! I know I had my last baby 10
years ago, but I might still pee my pants.

                    MOM
I know it's not easy Jess. It shouldn't be
easy. Anything worthwhile in life is usually a
big pain in the ass, too.

                  JESSICA
Now, there's a bumper sticker.

                    MOM
I still think there should be a third sex.

                  JESSICA
A third sex?

                    MOM
A third sex. Men don't fulfill all of our
emotional needs.

                    JENNY
Clearly.

                    MOM
And while I can see its merits, not every
woman wants be a lezzzzzbian.

JESSICA and JENNY are stifling their laughter.

MOM (cont'd)
There needs to be a third sex. A third option.

                    JENNY
There is, Mom, it's called single, with a
dildo.

                JESSICA AND MOM
JENNY!

They laugh. All three stop walking, pause to
look at each other a moment, and just smile.

                    JENNY
              (looks at watch)
God, I'm so late, I have to go.

Thanks for watching the boys tonight, Mom.

She hugs her mom and looks at JESSICA.

                    JENNY
Call me.

She leaves. Their MOM takes JESSICA's hand for
a moment as they sit on a fountain wall.

                    MOM
You know what to do, Jess. Write from your
heart. I always said you were going to do
something really very different.

                  JESSICA
Well, hell, Mum, you must be proud, this whole
scenario is pretty God damned different.

                    MOM
Don't over think it dear. Just get writing.

INT-JESSICA'S OFFICE-DAY

It's the next morning. JESSICA is standing in
front of her office window. Rousing, joyful
music starts playing over footage of her
looking outside at all the beauty, then
sitting at her desk to work away at her
manuscript, then beautiful, poignant footage
of her life as a Mommy: battling flu bugs,
disciplining, hugging and being playful with
her children.

                    JESSICA (V/O)
Someday, I'll miss this chaos. Someday, I'll
miss the grossness of it all: the wiping of
little bums and snotty noses; the Puke, Puke,
Everywhere Puke, because along with the putrid
comes loveliness: the unconditional love of
butterfly kisses, of warm, unending hugs; of a
small, sticky hand inside mine. Someday, I'll
miss the impossibly early mornings, the
insanely late nights, the flu bug the entire
family battles. I'll miss all the things I say
all-too-often: Don't hit. Don't shove. Share
your toys. Eat your breakfast. Be good now. Do
you have to go pee? No dessert until you eat
your supper. Brush your teeth. It's bedtime!
No. No. I said No. Because I Said So! Someday,
I'll want it all back. The thousands of
digital photos and movies won't do this
beautiful chaos any justice. The time is now,
and it is fleeting. So when this chaos has
disappeared from my life, this chaos I
complain about a little every day, I will
mourn for it with all my heart. I will mourn
for what I had but didn't always embrace. I
will mourn for what has flown away, for what
has evolved into something even greater; into
something I can only dream about. Someday,

I'll miss this beautiful chaos.

INT-JESSICA'S OFFICE-DAY

Dusk covers the room. Music that conjures up
feelings about the fragility of life and how
quickly time passes plays as JESSICA writes.
She sits back and reads what's on her screen.
She looks very emotional but pleased with what
she's written.

INT-JESSICA'S OFFICE-NIGHT TO DAY

The music continues playing as JESSICA writes
into the night and the wee small hours of the
morning.
She writes on a notepad at her desk, crumpling
up papers, and tries again. The backyard scene
outside her office window gradually changes
from summer to fall.

EXT-A NY CITY BOOKSTORE WINDOW-DAY

JESSICA and ALEXIS see their reflections in
the window; behind them are brilliant colored
fall trees. JESSICA looks at a book in the
window about writing novels. They go inside
together and come out with bags of books.
ALEXIS pulls her next door to a shoe store
window, they jump up and down as they point to
various shoes. They go inside and come out
wearing new shoes, skipping arm in arm,
looking refreshed and delighted.

Leaves are falling outside the office window.
JESSICA is at her desk dressed only in a white
towel, just out of the shower, typing up a
storm into her manuscript. BRIAN enters,

kisses her neck, tries to get her upstairs to
the bedroom. She stands to hug him. He tries
to take off her towel and gestures to the
bedroom. She is distracted, sensing the kids
coming into the room, and pushes him away,
shaking her head no, just as LILY and ELLA
enter the office together and go right to
their mother, tugging at her towel.

In slow motion, in time to the music, they are
broken apart, pulled in different directions
away from each other, a look of longing, of
loneliness, on their faces.

He opens his cell phone as he moves apart from
her; his wife is once again pulled away by
their children.

EXT-BOULDER BACKYARD -INT-JESSICA'S OFFICE
WINDOW-DAY

BRIAN is in the yard raking leaves and
mulching the grass with a lawn mover. JESSICA
is receiving an email from JACK. She's
laughing so hard she's almost crying. BRIAN
looks to the window at her chatting online
with longing, as he passes by with the mower,
a look of sadness and loneliness passes across
his eyes. We move through the window to inside
the room and see her close her email and open
the discussion forum page to talk with her
friends online. The music fades.

INT-JESSICA'S OFFICE-DAY

Sunshine fills the room. JESSICA looks vibrant
and relaxed. She talks as she types.

JESSICA

Last night I dreamed Nathan Lane hit on me at a party. I dream weird things when I don't get to sleep until 4 a.m. This novel won't let me sleep, it keeps wanting to be written!

INT-FRANK'S LIVING ROOM-DAY

FRANK is in his living room. The house is clean, and he looks happy and younger. His face is clean shaven.

                    FRANK
                 (laughing)
You keep on writing, girl. But Nathan Lane?

INT-JACK VENTURE'S L.A. MANSION-DAY
JACK is on his bed again, laptop once again in crotch, but this time he's wearing a bathrobe and green socks--with holes in them.

                    JACK
Do you regularly dream about famous actors flirting with you?

INT-JESSICA'S OFFICE-DAY

                    JESSICA
          (pauses to think, then types)
Oh yes. I like to keep things interesting, so I go through the alphabet of famous actors every month. Tonight, all the P's are getting lucky.

INT-JACK VENTURE'S L.A. MANSION-DAY

                    JACK
I've just decided to change my name to Peter Piper.

c/o JESSICA mixed with c/o JENNY mixed with
c/o FRANK mixed with c/o ALEXIS laughing so
hard and Diet Coke liquid is coming out of
ALEXIS's nose. JESSICA, JENNY, FRANK, ALEXIS
and JACK grin and sigh happily, then all
except JESSICA close their laptops.

INT-JESSICA'S OFFICE-NIGHT

JESSICA has been instant messaging ALEXIS.

                    JESSICA
Break a leg!

                    ALEXIS (V/0)
Thanks hun.

JESSICA starts to log off IM Chat when there's
a ping sound - there's a new message from
JACK. When she looks up, JACK's sitting on her
sofa in her office. He's got a tennis racket
in his hand and he looks fit and accomplished.
He grins at her.

                    JACK
You're not like other women, are you?

JESSICA reads her computer screen, and then
looks over at him.

                    JESSICA
Why do you say that?

                    JACK
You're not afraid to be yourself. To mean what
you say, and say what you mean.

                    JESSICA
Oh, I haven't always been this brave. I think
it comes from having children.

                    JACK
You have to be brave with your kids?

                    JESSICA
Oh yeah. They're like animals. They can smell

fear.

                    JACK
See if it were me, I'd be eaten alive. I think
you're doing an impressive job at it.

                    JESSICA
At parenthood, or at being myself?

                    JACK
Oh, at pretty much everything.

                    JESSICA
Are we flirting again?

                    JACK
Just a little bit. You're married. I wouldn't
want you to think I'm a creep.

                    JESSICA
I don't. I'm loving all this attention from
you.

                    JACK
See there you go again, saying it like it is.
Brave.

JESSICA
Ha. I don't know if that's brave or stupid.

                    JACK
It's admirable. If you're ever in LA, it would
be nice to meet for drinks.

JESSICA sits back and thinks about that for a
minute.

                    JESSICA
Why me?

                         JACK
Why not? You're more interesting than most of
my fangirls.

                       JESSICA
Don't call me a fangirl again, and maybe I'll
say yes.

                         JACK
I'm not sure if that's a maybe or a yes.

                       JESSICA
It's a "we'll see."

                         JACK
I'd throw in some Spiderman moves.

                       JESSICA
Well then, it's more like a maybe.

                         JACK
You're impossible.

JESSICA leans forward towards him.

                       JESSICA
I've been called an experience.

JACK leans forward towards her.

                         JACK
That you are.

JESSICA leans back in her chair looks at him
one more time, then turns her head to her
computer and types.

                         JESSICA
                       Bye, Jack.

FX: JESSICA closes her laptop, looking flushed
and excited, and JACK fades off the sofa as
she leaves the room.

INT-JESSICA AND BRIAN'S MASTER BATHROOM-NIGHT

JESSICA is in the shower, water spraying on
her back. Sexy music plays; it fits her V.O
and the sounds of the shower perfectly. She's
facing the wall with her hands above her head
- it's very sexy, like she's been handcuffed.
She rests her head on the shower wall gently,
and when her head turns we see a sexy smile on
her face.

                       JESSICA (V/O)
When our bodies were tangled like that; when
you touched me there, like that...fire.

We follow her as she gets out of the shower
dripping wet, wraps a towel around her, and
practically runs from the bathroom to her
office to her laptop to type her thoughts,

"When our bodies were tangled like that,"
furiously into her manuscript, titled, THE
FRIENDS I'VE NEVER MET. After a few minutes of
typing, she writes THE END and grins.

She prints the manuscript out and sits down on
the sofa beside her on her desk, then starts
to read it through, but falls asleep mid-way
through.

INT-JESSICA AND BRIAN'S BEDROOM-DAY

It's very early--the house is quiet. BRIAN is
quietly packing a suitcase. He packs his
laptop and manuscripts and checks his plane
ticket. But most of the time he's simply
kissing JESSICA on the forehead, brushing some
hair out of her eyes very tenderly and slowly,
smiling as he watches her sleep. He checks the
time on his phone.

INT-JESSICA'S OFFICE-DAY

BRIAN is in search of a pen and paper to write
JESSICA a note. He finds some yellow sticky
notes and starts to write, "I'll miss you," on
one. As he's writing it he sees the words THE
END on the manuscript on the sofa where
JESSICA left it. He does a double take, a
moment of recognition passes across his face;
and his expression turns to regret. He picks
up the manuscript and begins to read it. He's
spellbound.

INT-JESSICA'S OFFICE-DAY

A fun love song with an upbeat rhythm starts
to play. An hour has passed. BRIAN is writing
a new sticky note. He keeps it in his hand,
looks at the time on his phone, and rushes out
of the house.

EXT-STREETS OUTSIDE BOULDER HOME-DAY
It's very early. The neighborhood is still
asleep. BRIAN walks briskly to the 24-hr.
corner store.

INT-CORNER STORE-DAY

BRIAN spends some time picking out a chocolate

bar.

INT-BOULDER HOME-DAY

BRIAN returns, closes the door quietly, and
rushes up the stairs.

INT-JESSICA'S OFFICE-DAY

BRIAN puts the chocolate on the manuscript and
leaves it beside her computer keyboard. And
then the note.

                    BRIAN (V/O)
Jess, this is fantastic. I was wrong, I can be
both. I should be both. I'm going to send it
out. ~Your loving agent.

BRIAN rushes out the room, grabs his suitcase,
and goes down the stairs.

EXT-BOULDER HOME-DAY

BRIAN gets in the taxi that's waiting on the
driveway. As it drives away, his expression is
hopeful as he looks back over his shoulder,
through the back window.

INT-JESSICA'S OFFICE-DAY

Just as the V.O. ends, Sammy the fat tabby cat
jumps up onto the desk and munches through the
paper and tinfoil wrapping to eat the dark
chocolate. The note falls ever so slowly, like
a leaf, to the floor and under her desk, never
to be found. The song ends.

INT-JESSICA AND BRIAN'S ROOM

An alarm goes off--8. a.m. JESSICA wakes up to
roll into her husband and cuddle him, only to
find him not there. She feels around for his
body, opens her eyes, then there's recognition
on her face.

She gets out of bed slowly and heads

downstairs.

JESSICA'S OFFICE-DAY

JESSICA walks into her office, sits down, and
finds some chocolate that's been chewed on on
her desk and the remains on the floor. Her
manuscript is also in a mess on the floor.

                    JESSICA
What?

She calls down the stairs.

                    JESSICA (CONT')
Aidan, what have I told you about using my
desk without asking!

She lets out a frustrated sigh when she
doesn't hear AIDAN respond--she can hear the
kids listening to cartoons downstairs in the
family room. She tidies up her manuscript and
the chocolate wrapper, and leaves the office
in a bad mood. The little love note is just
lying there on the floor under her computer
desk, unread.

INT-FRANK'S LIVING ROOM - JERSEY CITY -NIGHT

JENNY and FRANK and ALEXIS and JESSICA are
sitting back, watching a Jack Venture movie
with popcorn, beers, sodas--the works. JESSICA
feels her cell phone vibrate. She's received a
text. She sees JACK's name and reads it, then
whispers to ALEXIS, who's beside her.

                    JESSICA
It's Jack. He's shooting a film in Manhattan.
He wants to meet me for drinks.

                    ALEXIS
Are you freaking out?

                    JESSICA
Just a little. He's as famous as Doug Evan!

                    ALEXIS
Um, more famous. Doug became old news when
Hannah Storm left him for that sexy Tripp
Wilson, the bird dude. Come to think of it,
I've read Hannah, Tripp and Jack are friends.

                    JESSICA
Why does any of this matter?

JESSICA

I suppose it doesn't. I'm nervous babbling for
you. Ask Jack to call you!

JESSICA texts back. His reply pops up:

JACK (V.O).

I can't do that right now. Let's just meet
tomorrow night. By now FRANK and JENNY know
something is going on. Everyone is crowded
around JESSICA, who's sitting on the sofa in
shock. She texts a response.

JESSICA

So I'm supposed to just show up somewhere and
get murdered?

ALEXIS takes her arm beside her on the sofa.
JENNY and FRANK are just behind them, on pins
and needles, too. Everyone is holding their
breath waiting for his response. JACK's reply
pops up on the cell a second later.

JACK (V/O.)

I'd never ask you to just show up somewhere.
You'll be picked up in a limo, and taken to
the Carlyle. I'm in the Empire Suite. I'll
make dinner reservations for 8:00. After that,
we could go for a walk in Central Park.

JENNY

Good Lord, a man who plans ahead. God must
have broken the mould.

JESSICA

It does sound really romantic.

ALEXIS

Like out of a movie.

                    JENNY
One of those movie moments you're always
talking about. Now here's your chance.

                    FRANK
If you don't go, I will.

                    JESSICA
What are you people smoking! I'm married!

                    JENNY
You're not dead.

                    JESSICA
I might be. After I do this. I might be.

                    JENNY
It's just drinks.

                    ALEXIS
It could be a business opportunity, too.

                    JESSICA
I'm sure he's got business on his mind.

ALEXIS has turned giddy. She's lost in the
romance of it all.

                    ALEXIS
Just meet him for drinks. You can use my place
to get ready. He can pick you up there. Do it!

                    JESSICA
But..the kids...Brian's away on business...

                    JENNY
Mom will take care of everyone. And it's
Steve's weekend with the boys. I'll help get

you ready.

ALEXIS and JENNY are ecstatic now. It's like
it's already decided.

                    JESSICA
Well, ...

                    FRANK
Remember? Thoreau? How can you be a writer if
you haven't lived?

                    JESSICA
Aren't we taking what Thoreau meant just a
little too far?

                    FRANK
Maybe, just a little. But it's one of those
stretches that feels reaaaaaaal good.

JESSICA looks at them all like she can't win.
She can't fight this any longer. She texts
JACK. "I'll be there." A moment later she's
reading his response on her cell.

                    JACK (V/O)
Great. I'll have a car sent for you. Can't
wait.

                    JESSICA
Now there's a big problem. BIG. BIG PROBLEM.

                    JENNY
Oh no, what?

                    JESSICA
I have kick ass shoes, but nothing to wear.

She looks at FRANK. He has a hopeful look on

his face.

                    JESSICA (cont'd)
No, I won't go naked.

                    FRANK
Fair enough. I thought there was a two percent
chance.

                    JESSICA
Not even.

                    JENNY
So you know what this means then?

They all look at each other.

                    LADIES
SHOPPING TRIP!

FRANK rolls his eyes.

EXT -NEW YORK -MANHATTAN-DAY.

Fun, upbeat music plays as the group walks
around Time Square. They are all high on
friendship and everything New York.

INT-MANHATTAN DRESS STORE-DAY

FRANK is sitting on a bench, waiting
patiently. ALEXIS and JENNY come out of a
change room, followed by JESSICA in a lovely,
conservative top and jeans.

                    FRANK
Big thumbs down. I see no speed bumps.

JESSICA comes out next in a stunning, low cut
blouse and dress pants.

                    FRANK (cont'd)
That could kill a man. But, good luck to him.

He gives it a big thumbs up.

The music gets louder and ties in with footage
of the friends having fun in Manhattan. They
get silly modeling outfits. The girls get
their makeup done at Macy's, and try to put
lipstick on FRANK, but he won't have any of it
At the end of the day they hang out in Central
Park near a water fountain. They all jump in
the fountain, fully clothed, and FRANK takes
pictures of them goofing around. The last shot
in this scene is from above, all of them
laughing, circled around JESSICA as she
twirls. She looks sexy, vibrant. The music
plays out, tying this section together.

INT-ALEXIS'S NY APARTMENT-NIGHT

ALEXIS is doing JESSICA's hair. She turns
JESSICA around in her chair. She's in a
cocktail dress that's super short and
psycadelic 70s print - it looks a little young
for her. Her breasts are at least one cup size

bigger and her hair is very badly crimped and teased. JENNY holds up a mirror for her.

                    JESSICA
I look like Dolly Parton and Lyle Lovett's love child.

                    ALEXIS
Ok, so the crimping iron didn't work very well. I thought it would look young and fun.

                    JESSICA
My hair is the least of my problems Alex. My
boobs are a couple of lighthouse beacons.

                     JENNY
Yea, they're beacons alright, beckoning any
and all New York sailors home. All aboard!

                    JESSICA
Stop it. Do I look okay?

                     JENNY
It's just the dress. And the hair. Ok, it's
everything. Come on, we can fix this.

The three girls go into the bathroom.

EXT-MANHATTAN-CARLYLE HOTEL-NIGHT

Traffic and people are bustling around the
hotel.

INT-MANHATTAN-CARLYLE HOTEL-EMPIRE SUITE-NIGHT

JACK Venture is sitting on a king size bed in
his boxers and holey socks again. He's talking
on a cell phone, laughing.

                     JACK
Okay, I have that one thing to do first, and
then I can meet you. Yeah, I can't wait
either. See you then.

JACK checks the time on his phone, then puts
the phone to sleep and sets it down on a side
table. He looks
a wide, full length mirror beside the bed, and
stares at his own image for a while.

                              JACK
Dude, don't screw this up.

"Macho man" begins to play. JACK gets up and
starts flexing his muscles to the words "Body
body, wanna touch my body baby," puts on the
shirt that's lying neatly on the bed, then
puts on the pants one leg at a time, tripping
a little as he tries to dress. He puts on a
nice matching suit jacket. He combs his hair
fastidiously and checks for stuff in his
teeth. He does a few poses, trying to see what
pose looks the most macho. Then he actually
gives himself an emphatic thumbs up sign and
winks. The music stops abruptly.

                              JACK
Nah, no, nuh-huh, that would be wrong.

He tries two thumbs up. When he sees how he
looks in the mirror his expression turns to
embarrassment. He points his fingers like
guns, spins around and shoots the mirror; then
stops in his tracks and sticks out his tongue-
-far, far out in frustration.

                              JACK
GAHHHHHH! This Sexiest Man Alive thing is
going to kill me. I can't live up to this.
It's like standing in traffic!

He bangs his head against the mirror. His eyes
slowly roll upward to meet their sad, sorry
excuse for a reflection. There's a knock at
his bedroom door.

                              JACK
Yeah Kimberly, it's okay, come in.

Jack's assistant KIMBERLY pokes her head around his door.

                    KIMBERLY
Jack, your 7 p.m. is waiting downstairs, should I show him in? You're running a few minutes behind schedule.

                    JACK
Sure. I'll be out in a minute.

Kimberly nods and leaves, closing the door again.

                    JACK
Get yourself together Jack. GET YOURSELF TOGETHER! You are not a wuss. You're the man. And she likes you. She really likes you! You'll shake her hand, and take it from there. You can do this.

He looks at his watch, sighs, then turns toward the window and leans one hand and his head against it, looking out at the city lights.

INT-ALEXIS'S APARTMENT-NIGHT

FRANK has one hand and his head against the glass, and is gazing out the window at the city lights, too. After a few seconds he looks at his watch, turns and goes to knock on ALEXIS's bedroom door. ALEXIS answers.

                    FRANK
You ladies almost ready?

His jaw drops when JESSICA enters the room in an elegant, low cut long black dress, 1940s movie-glam, sexy elegance. Her hair is no longer crimped, it's flowing to her shoulders.

                    FRANK
Wow, you're smokin!

He is looking over at JENNY, not just at JESSICA. After a minute he diverts his attention back to JESSICA.

                    FRANK
He'd better not be a prick.

JESSICA looks over at her sister.

                    JESSICA
Or an ass monkey.

                    FRANK
Right. Pricks and ass monkeys don't deserve women in dresses like that. Are you ready?

FRANK puts out his arm for JESSICA.

                    FRANK (cont'd)
Allow me to escort you downstairs, Madame. Jack's limo will be here for you soon.

JESSICA takes a deep breath and shakes her head. She sits down on the sofa and takes her cell phone out of her small purse.

                    JESSICA
I can't do this. As much as he's a clueless Neanderthal at times, I really love my husband.

ALEXIS and JENNY come up behind the sofa and

realize she's about to text JACK.

ALEXIS
No. Oh, no. Don't send that text, Jess. You'll
always wonder about tonight. Just go and meet
Jack.
It's just drinks.

JENNY takes the phone from her sister's hands.

JENNY
I think you need to do this.

JESSICA shakes her head.

JESSICA
All I needed was New York. I feel new again.

FRANK
Just go meet him. The guy sent a stretch limo
for you, for God's sake. You can't pass that
up.

He pushes her toward the door. They go down
the elevator together. JESSICA hugs her sister
and both her friends in front of the limo, and
gets in. Her expression is both unsure, and
excited.

EXT-STREETS OF MANHATTAN-NIGHT

The song "Wild Women Do' by Natalie Cole plays
as limo goes through the streets of Manhattan.

EXT-CARLYLE HOTEL-NIGHT

The music changes -something big is about to
happen. The limo arrives in front of the hotel
and the driver helps JESSICA out. She looks

like a movie star arriving at
a premiere.

INT-CARLYLE HOTEL ELEVATOR-NIGHT

JESSICA is biting her nails. The elevator
opens right into the Empire Suite.

INT-EMPIRE SUITE-NIGHT

JESSICA looks around. It's breathtaking. After
a moment, she sees JACK's back. He's wearing a
very nice suit, the same suit from when he was
getting ready earlier in the hotel. He's still
looking out the window, his back to her.
JESSICA looks at him for a moment from behind,
and glances down at her wedding band. She
starts fiddling with it as she turns and
begins to walk briskly away, tears welling in
her eyes, her expression turning to regret,
then mild panic. She darts for the elevator
and pushes the button quickly, a couple times,
trying to leave without being heard.

JACK hears her and turns around quickly. Only
it's not JACK. It's her husband BRIAN. He
starts to run after her before she gets in the
elevator.

                    BRIAN
Jess, don't leave, don't leave!

JESSICA stops in her tracks, slowly turns
around inside the elevator, and looks up at
her husband with shock on her face. He's
firmly holding the elevator door open with his
hand and arm to keep it from closing.

                    JESSICA

It was you. It was you? This whole time?

                    BRIAN
Jess, it's always been me.

                    JESSICA
Always?

                    BRIAN
After Frank took his wife off life support...

                    JESSICA
Oh God. That hit you too.

JESSICA walks out of the elevator and closer
to her husband.

He takes her hands in his.

                    BRIAN
Of course it did. Of course.

                    JESSICA
You didn't tell me.

                    BRIAN
We weren't connecting. So I tried something
different.

                    JESSICA
Holy crap.

                    BRIAN
It was Venture on the public fan page, me in
the emails and texts.

                    JESSICA
Holy crap!

                              BRIAN
I wanted to give you the romance you wanted.

                             JESSICA
All these months?

                              BRIAN
I wanted to give you something out of the
ordinary.

C/o of JESSICA's face as she begins to put
everything together, realizing it was her
husband turning her on, making her laugh.

                           DISSOLVE TO

INT -BRIAN'S CAR -DAY

We see BRIAN in a suit in a traffic jam,
texting her the words "Why are women like you
always married?"

INT- JESSICA'S OFFICE-DAY

We see JESSICA's flattered reaction when she
initially read that sentence.

EXT -PARK BENCH -DAY

BRIAN is in a suit one workday lunchtime,
beside a lake on a park bench, typing on a
laptop - we read the words he'd written:
"JESSICA, you could write anything you want,
so get to it." We see the words ANYTHING YOU
WANT up close.

INT- JESSICA'S OFFICE -DAY

JESSICA takes off her glasses, sits back and
smiles. She is beginning to believe in herself
again.

                                      BACK TO
INT -EMPIRE SUITE-NIGHT

                    BRIAN
I know I don't seem like the same exciting guy
who took you to Paris at the spur of the
moment in our 20s. Paying bills and
renegotiating the mortgage wore me down a
little. But I still feel the very same way I
did then.

                    JESSICA
You do?

                    BRIAN
Of course I do. Maybe our life is kind of
ordinary, but together, we're extraordinary.

JESSICA is still in shock. She's piecing
everything
together. It leaves her breathless.

                    JESSICA

Everything you wrote...it was so...romantic.

                    BRIAN
I meant it all. All of it. Maybe it's corny,
but I feel this ...fire... when we're
together.

                    JESSICA
          (Walks toward him, tears in
                    eyes)
I feel it too. But, when our crazy life gets
in the way, it's always me putting the fire
back on.

                         BRIAN
Not this time.

He wraps his arms around her and grins.

                         BRIAN
         (laughs and holds up his cell phone)
This time I got you hot, baby! In an
unconventional way...

                        JESSICA
Ya think?

                         BRIAN
It *was* kind of insane.

JESSICA looks around the room, lifts up the
long skirt of her beautiful gown.

                        JESSICA
And I fell for it.

                         BRIAN
I don't blame you. Every woman deserves to
feel like a princess.

                        JESSICA
Okay, what the hell have you been reading?

                         BRIAN
Not reading, playing. Lily and Ella took me
hostage while you were away. Aidan ran away to
his friend's house, but it was too late for
me.

                        JESSICA
Tiara?

                    BRIAN
Yup.

                   JESSICA
Heels?

                    BRIAN
Oh, yeah.

                   JESSICA
Not my good ones!

                    BRIAN
Never.

                   JESSICA
I really love you, you know. I wasn't going to
sleep with him. I was just ... kind of
curious.

                    BRIAN
Oh, so all this, and I'm not getting laid?

                   JESSICA
Oh, you're getting laid, husband. Just look at
this place!

She looks around at the gorgeous Suite.

                   JESSICA
How did you pull this off?

                    BRIAN
He knows you from the group page. Not your
blog or emails, that was all me, but
everything you wrote on the page impressed
him, and he remembered your name. I called his
studio.

                    JESSICA
You spoke with Jack Venture?

                    BRIAN
It took 15 calls before he actually spoke with
me. Your manuscript is genius, sweetie. I'm
sorry I didn't read it before I did.

JESSICA has lost her breath again.

                    JESSICA
What? My new manuscript?

                    BRIAN
Yea, the one you said wasn't good enough. A
few weeks ago, I sent it to him. I told him
I'm your agent. I should have been your agent
a long time ago.

                    JESSICA
My agent?

                    BRIAN
I know it's not even published yet, but he's
interested in getting it made into a movie. He
put us up in this room. We're meeting with his
people tomorrow.

                    JESSICA
You're not serious.

                    BRIAN
Would I lie to you?

                    JESSICA
Uh, yea, try, online, for three months!

                         BRIAN
How could I stop? I could tell it was driving
your writing.

                        JESSICA
                        (softly)
You inspired me. You woke something up inside
me.

                         BRIAN
Good. You woke something up inside me.

                        JESSICA
Don't be a jerk now and make it about that. I
meant emotionally.

                         BRIAN
I know. But the flirting was fun, right?

                        JESSICA
Except for the part where I thought I was
going to have a coronary reading what he
wrote, and what I typed back to him - I mean
to you - yes.

                         BRIAN
So you'll keep me?

                        JESSICA
I think so. Let's see how rich I get first. I
may not need your services after that.

                         BRIAN
Oh, no? Speaking of services, I think we have
some business to take care of. I'm your acting
manager now. I demand to be paid.

He pushes her down on bed and kisses her
passionately. It's very sexy. She's not

complaining.

                    BRIAN
I love you. You need to know that.

JESSICA sits up mid-way again, glances at her
wedding ring, ponders it sadly.

                    JESSICA
I knew that. GOD. I am such an idiot.

                    BRIAN
Maybe, just a little bit. But you're MY idiot.

JESSICA grins, wipes a tear from her eye,
kisses him again.

                    JESSICA
You know, when you were Venture, you told me
you liked sushi. I never knew you liked sushi.

                    BRIAN
And I never knew you were such a sex kitten.
Some of your thoughts are down-right slutty
aren't they?

                    JESSICA
Stay awake one of these nights and I'll show
you slutty.

                    BRIAN
               (feeling her hips slowly)
At this moment, I am very awake. You. Are. A.
Goddess.

He gives her the 'One minute" sign with his
finger.

                    BRIAN

Just a sec.

He walks over toward a stereo, picks up the
remote, clicks ON. A beautiful, perfectly
danceable love song starts to play.

                    BRIAN (cont'd)
We can't waste perfectly good, clean-up-nicely
clothes.

He holds out his hand, and she takes it.

                    JESSICA
That would be wrong.

They dance together ballroom style as though
they've done it as dance partners for decades.
They are smooth and relaxed. It's beautiful.
It's a modern day Cinderella. The music plays
for a good minute before JESSICA speaks.

                    JESSICA
Smooth. Very smooth. But don't think this gets
you off the hook.

                    BRIAN
For what?

                    JESSICA
    I still I want my fancy dinner and walk in
                Central Park.

                    BRIAN
We can do that every night for a week. Your
Mom's watching the kids.

                    JESSICA
So sex, more sex, then sushi?

                          BRIAN
You're such a romantic.

JESSICA laughs as BRIAN twirls her around in
time to the music. Mixed with this scene, we
are shown several flashback scenes that show
that all along it was BRIAN, not JACK, sending
her emails and making her feel good about
herself, and we see the strong connection this
husband and wife always had. Something
beautiful plays over the footage, tying
everything together (Van Morrison, Someone
Like You).

INT-EMPIRE SUITE -NIGHT

JESSICA and BRIAN are rolling in bed in the
beautiful suite, laughing and kissing
passionately. The song plays out until the
end.

INT-CARLYLE HOTEL LOBBY -NIGHT

FRANK, ALEXIS and JENNY get out of a taxi cab,
wearing dressy clothes, and enter the hotel
lobby. They look around, then look at the
elevators and what floor they're coming from.
ALEXIS is beside herself; JENNY and FRANK a
little calmer.

                          ALEXIS
Oh my God. It's coming down from the Empire
Suite. It's gotta be him. He's meeting US.
WE'RE going to meet Jack Venture. Jack
Venture, who works with some of the most
powerful people in Hollywood. Steven
Spielberg. Tom Hanks. Oh my freaking God. Do I
look okay? Is there anything in my teeth?

                         JENNY
Alex, calm down. Put on your big girl panties.
You don't think Tom Hanks has boogers like the
rest of us?

                         FRANK
Good point Jen. But I'll bet he uses those 3-
ply tissues with the moisturizer in them.

                         ALEXIS
I'm fine guys, I'm just really excited. I
really like him.

                         FRANK
Really? Shocker. You fooled us there.

                         JENNY
He's just a guy, Alex. He's just a guy.

The elevator door opens and JACK walks out,
beaming at his three online friends. JENNY
takes a step back. She stops breathing. Her
eyes get big as JACK walks down a long
corridor toward them.

                    JENNY (cont'd)
                      (whispers)
Holy freaking honey nut bunches of oats, it's
really him. I think I'm gonna throw up. Or
faint.

FRANK gets behind her to hold her up a little.

                         FRANK
                      (whispers)
What happened to he's just a guy? And what's
with the breakfast cereals as curse words?

                    JENNY
                  (whispers)
Not just cereals, breakfast foods. It's
something new I'm trying, for the sake of my
kids.

                   ALEXIS
Frosted fucking flakes he's hot.

                    JENNY
                  (whispers)
Yea, uh, that's not really how ...

FX: JENNY is interrupted by JACK who, in slow
motion, is walking straight toward her. He has
a bright, confident smile on his face, and
looks very suave and sophisticated. Suddenly,
he trips on his own shoelace. He falls to the
floor in even slower motion.

                    JACK
ARGHHHHHHHHHHHHHHH-BUGGER-ALL-DAMN-IT-FUCK-
NUTS!

ALEXIS gasps. JENNY just stands there, hands
over her mouth.

Frank runs right over to him, and looks at his
legs. He sees Jack moving to get up.

                   FRANK
                (helping him up)
You're okay?

                    JACK
Yeah, yeah I'm fine. Stepped on my damned
glasses though. Again.

He takes a pair of glasses from under his shoe and holds them up. They're completely crushed.

                    FRANK
Nice job. The stores are still open. We could go glasses shopping right now...

                    JACK
          (laughs as he takes Frank's
           hand and gets up off the
                    ground)
God no, they're just for fashion. And that's what Bev in props is for. She's used to me.

                    FRANK
Ah. So you planned that entrance, right?

                    JACK
Of course. More memorable this way. Don't worry, in order to get my pride back, I'll just sue the hotel.

FRANK laughs. JACK grins and shakes FRANKS's hand. He brushes off his pants, then quickly turns to JENNY who's got her hands over her mouth.

                    JACK
Jenny right? I recognize you from your photo, and you look like your sister.

JENNY slowly lowers one hand to shake his hand, as the other arm falls limp to her side. Now her mouth is completely wide open, but she says nothing. She's in a star-struck daze.

                    FRANK
Was Jess surprised? She wasn't angry with us, was she?

                          JACK
Oh no, she was completely, happily surprised.

                          FRANK
Good.

                          JACK
I popped in and they were drinking champagne.
I thought I should leave them be, but it was
fun to meet her.

                          FRANK
I can't believe you gave them your suite.

                          JACK
Yea well I have the whole floor beneath it. No
worries.

                          FRANK
You're a romantic at heart.

                          JACK
I'm a sucker for romantic stories. Plus, I'd
like them in a good mood for negotiations
tomorrow.

ALEXIS laughs, a little too hard.

                          ALEXIS
HA! We helped, you know.

                          JACK
Oh, I know. You guys are the biggest mischief
makers in the group.
                      (beat)

                  JACK (CONT')

So. Alexis. We finally meet.

They shake hands, and keep holding hands for
more than necessary. Their eyes connect. It's
electric.

FRANK ushers motionless, speechless JENNY over
to a sofa in the lobby and sits her down,
trying to stifle his laughter over her star
struck condition. JACK's gaze is only on
ALEXIS. She plays with her neck and collar
bone nervously.

                    ALEXIS
So. Here we are.

                    JACK
Here we are.

                    ALEXIS
No computer screens between us.

                    JACK
Not one.

                    ALEXIS
That's okay right?

                    JACK
That's very okay. Why don't we all go
somewhere and talk in person?

                    ALEXIS
That would be great. Hey, I know this great
dance club...

FRANK hears her and walks over and interjects.

                              FRANK
God no Alex, we just met the nice man, let's
not kill him our first night out.

JACK looks amused.

                               JACK
We can go anywhere you want.

                              ALEXIS
Maybe just a café for starters.

                               JACK
Coffee's great. Mocca double expresso right?

ALEXIS giggles and grins.

                              FRANK
Wonders of technology. We'd have never met you
without the Internet.

                               JACK
Oh I don't know. Some things are meant to be.

He looks over at ALEXIS and grins. The three
walk through the hotel doors outside to his
stretch limo out front.

EXT-FRONT OF CARLYLE HOTEL/INT-LIMO-NIGHT

FRANK motions to JENNY to come, and she
follows behind, still speechless. JACK notices
her state and helps her into the limo first,
then FRANK, and ALEXIS is left on the street
still, to his side.

JENNY is now grinning and playing with
buttons; checking out everything in the limo.

                         JENNY
Oh my pancakes! What does this do?

                         JACK
Oh my pancakes?

                        ALEXIS
Yea, about that, we're clearly demented. You
sure you want to hang with us?

                         JACK
Positive. I prefer demented. Demand it,
actually. It's in my friendship clause. You'll
have to sign that later.

JACK and ALEXIS look at each other and burst
into laughter. JACK's cell phone rings. ALEXIS
looks at JACK's pocket, then at him.

                        ALEXIS
Aren't you going to answer that?

JACK puts his hand on the small of her back
and gently helps her into the limo, getting in
with her.

                         JACK
Nah. Whoever it is can wait.

They smile at each other. JENNY has gotten
into the champagne and hands them each a
glass. All four clink glasses and grin at each
other.

                         ALL
Cheers!

                        FRANK
To friendship.

                    JACK
To *online* friendship.

                   ALEXIS
To a friend we've finally met.

                   JENNY
Oh, screw it, my kids aren't even here. Jack,
this is fucking fantastic!

They all laugh, start chatting and the women
start singing along as an upbeat song starts
to play.

EXT-RED CARPET AFFAIR IN NEW YORK CITY -
EVENING - 12 MONTHS LATER

It's a beautiful night for a red carpet movie
premiere. A limo pulls up in front of the red
carpet. JACK gets out and puts his hand out.
ALEXIS slowly gets out of the car and takes
JACK's hand. There are posters all around,
"THE FRIENDS I'VE NEVER MET" and JACK and
ALEXIS are front and center on them.

On the carpet, ALEXIS is beaming. She has
arrived where she always wanted to be. JACK
reaches for her hand and squeezes it, she
looks up to him for a minute and smiles. They
turn and applaud as another limo pulls up.
BRIAN gets out and puts out his hand to help
JESSICA out of the car. They look gorgeous.
They wave at JACK and ALEXIS, JESSICA gives
ALEXIS a little discreet thumbs up and a smirk
and ALEXIS moves in closer to JACK and grins.
Everyone laughs as BRIAN makes a big scene for
everyone and dips his wife on the red carpet.

EXT BOULDER HOME BACKYARD-DAY

The scene begins on a glorious fall day from a
tree above the backyard, then moves through a
kitchen window to inside the kitchen.

INT-KITCHEN-DAY

JESSICA is doing dishes. Supper is bubbling
slowly in a crock pot. The kitchen looks clean
and bright. JESSICA takes off her gloves and
dries her hands and looks out the kitchen
window to her family, a smile growing bigger
and bigger on her face.

EXT-BOULDER BACKYARD-EVENING

BRIAN has a football in his hand. He moves in
slow motion, falling to the ground with LILY,
now 5, ELLA, 7, and AIDAN, 11 - JESSICA closes
the back patio screen door, runs to her
family, catches the ball BRIAN throws her. He
tackles her and the kids all fall on top of
their parents, laughing.

                    JESSICA (V/O)
Through a window, wondering what it's all
about, I look outside and suddenly see it:
your feet dancing in the lush green grass,
their tiny legs, running fast to avoid
tickles, and when they're finally caught, the
sight of you falling together to the ground:
you laughing like a child again, them, laying
their head on your chest-- like it's where
they belong.

A joyful upbeat song plays over footage of
JESSICA and BRIAN playing together in the
leaves, throwing them at their children and
each other.

INT-FRANK'S KITCHEN-DAY

The music fades but continues lightly in the
background. FRANK is in a blue bathrobe,
relaxing at his breakfast table, reading the
last few words of JESSICA's latest novel NO
ORDINARY DAYS. The cover of the book reads:
FROM THE AUTHOR OF THE BEST-SELLING NOVEL AND
SCREENPLAY 'THE FRIENDS I'VE NEVER MET.' He's
reading with great interest and emotion.

                    JESSICA (V/O)
Through a window, standing back, these small

moments make everything clear.

As the credits begin rolling, FRANK starts
sobbing uncontrollably. He puts the book down
on the table, reaches for a napkin, and dabs
his eyes.

                    FRANK
                (still sniffling)
Good God, your sister has got to stop making
me cry like a baby. I'm a grown man!

JENNY, also wearing a bathrobe, saunters up
behind him, laughing. She places a plate of
bacon and eggs in front of him, puts her arms
around him from behind, kisses his neck, sits
down. He looks at her lovingly, dabs his eyes,
then starts laughing.

                    FRANK
Do you realize we're both wearing bathrobes?

                    JENNY
Ah, yes, I guess we are. I didn't want to be
flashing you my fat arse during breakfast.

                    FRANK
You're beautiful. More like I didn't want to
be flashing you mine. It's fat and hairy.

                JENNY (laughs)
EWW, not the image I want at breakfast, hon.
We're also chatting. We're having the chat.

                    FRANK
Nah. It doesn't count if there was any snoring
in between the sex and the chat.

                    JENNY
I do not snore!

                    FRANK
Jen, honey, I hate to tell you, but you snore.

                    JENNY
I'm taking back that breakfast.

FRANK gets up, swoops her up, carries her in
his arms out of the kitchen. She laughs but
doesn't protest.

                         FRANK
That's fine. Just don't take back you.

                         JENNY
                       (laughing)
Nice try, but I'm going to need a foot rub as
an apology. Hey, I wanted that toast! Hey!

The credits roll over them laughing together
as he carries her away, with the remainder of
the song playing out.

                       THE END

To read more of author Heather Grace Stewart's work, please visit her official website, http://heathergracestewart.com Sign up with one click for her Readers Club to learn first about exclusive book bargains and contests!

More Books By Heather Grace Stewart:

Strangely, Incredibly Good
Remarkably Great
The Ticket
Good Nights
Lauren from Last Night

The Groovy Granny
Where the Butterflies Go
Leap
Three Spaces
Caged: New and Selected Poems
Stargazing

Made in the USA
Monee, IL
09 June 2021